Gold Rush Bride Tegan

By Linda Shenton Matchett

Gold Rush Bride Tegan
By Linda Shenton Matchett

Copyright 2022 by Linda Shenton Matchett. All rights reserved.
Cover Design by: Wes Matchett
Scene Dividers: Pixabay/Gordon Johnson
Girl in Hat: Boiko Olha/Shutterstock; River: Sven Lachmann/Pixabay

ISBN-13: 978-1-7363256-9-8

Published by Shortwave Press

Dawson City, Yukon, Canada

June 1899

Chapter One

"There's gold to be had, I'm tellin' ya."

Elijah Hunter pricked up his ears as he surveyed the shelves of canned goods in the mercantile. He didn't recognize the voice, but that didn't mean anything. In the three and half years since his arrival, Dawson City had grown into a true city with over forty thousand residents. Only about half of those were prospectors, with the other half providing the support structures, including saloons, gambling houses, and dance halls.

His time in the Yukon had been fruitful, but he had been part of the initial influx of miners, when a man could show up with a horse, a trowel, a pan, and some food. His outlay had been minimal, and he'd reaped the rewards of a productive claim. By the time the stampede started in ninety-seven, the authorities had passed laws that required anyone arriving to bring at least a year's worth of food. Combined with their camping and mining gear, the prospectors were carrying nearly twelve hundred pounds of food and outlaying a hefty amount of cash to purchase the means to do so.

Despite the supplies brought in, prices of everything had skyrocketed with even a nag of a horse going for seven hundred dollars. At forty dollars a day, the rental cost was even worse. By all reports, the gold was beginning to play out, so either the man found a hidden vein or the glittering dust had been found somewhere else in North America.

The thought sent tingles up his spine. Riches were fine, and he wasn't going to turn up his nose at the amount of money he had sitting in the bank, thanks to his success, but searching for gold, proving he could best the earth by getting its rocks and rivers to give up their precious ore gave him a thrill like nothing else.

Heels banging against the wooden floor, he threaded his way through the shelves to where a scrawny man in rumpled clothes, hat pushed back on his greasy hair, leaned against the front counter. Surrounded by a half-dozen men, he tapped on the glass with a dirt-encrusted finger. "I've sold my claim and am headed south. Tomorrow. You gents should join me."

Elijah's left eyebrow shot up. "You sound pretty confident, Mr. ..."

"Bowman. Henry Bowman, and I am. My buddy is already down there raking in the gold. He said there's plenty to be had."

"And where exactly is *down there*?"

"Nome, Alaska." The man rocked on the balls of his feet. "I'll be glad to get out of this place. The Canadians never wanted us here, and we'll be back in the good ol' USA, well, a place we own, anyway."

"I'm going, too. I heard you can pick up the gold on the beach." A husky man with blond hair and pockmarks on his face crossed his arms. "Did your buddy say anything about that?"

Bowman frowned. "Where'd ya hear that?"

The man pulled out a crumpled piece of newspaper from his pocket and smoothed it on the counter. Stabbing at the headline, he looked smug. "In this article, and they was right about the Yukon, so I'm thinkin' they're right about this one."

"I've been to Baja, Cripple Creek, and Mount Baker, and gold is never that easy to find." Elijah shook his head. "You can't pluck it off the ground like fallen apples."

"You should listen to him, boys, Mr. Hunter here has done good in every one of them rushes he mentioned." Phineas Dennehey, the shopkeeper, pushed the paper back toward the blond man. "I'd take his advice over that of some reporter just tryin' to make a name for himself."

"Suit yourself." The man shrugged and stuffed the scrap into his pocket. "Leaves more gold for me."

"I'll go with you," the blond said.

"Yeah, me, too. I got nothin' left here." Another man piped up. "My claim hasn't produced hardly anything in weeks."

Elijah listened as the men talked among themselves, some skeptical, but most seemed eager to turn their backs on the Yukon and try their luck at another location. His own claim was still producing, but the excitement was gone. The days blurred in an endless succession of rising with the sun, making his way to the surging river, and hunching over the water swirling his pan. Dawson City was lawful, almost complacent being under the protection of the Canadian North-West Mounted Police. Gambling and prostitution were acceptable, and the lawmen kept the robbery and murder rates low. Because of the city's remoteness, communication with the outside world was scarce, with news and mail arriving sporadically, months after being sent.

He rubbed his jaw. Perhaps it was time to seek a new opportunity. Biding his time until the crowd dispersed, he prowled through the mercantile weighing the pros and cons of pulling up stakes and starting fresh.

"I see yer thinkin' of leavin town." Phineas appeared around the edge of one of the displays. "You've got that look in yer eye."

"You know me well, my friend." Elijah grinned at the man. "I'm still making money, so that's not the issue."

"Nope. You're bored." The shopkeeper glanced over his shoulder, then leaned close. "But I've heard enough griping that the claims are drying up. It's probably time for you to move on. Me, too, but I'll wait a bit longer."

Elijah cocked his head. "Why wait?"

"As long as there are miners comin' in, I can earn a living, and I'd rather close up at the end of the season. I won't do another winter here." He rubbed his hands together, his eyes sparkling. "But then I'm headin' to Texas to do some ranching." His face pinked. "I've been correspondin' with a widow woman down there. I'm tired of bein' cold, but mostly, I'm tired of being lonely. There're no women up here."

"Well, there are, but not the marrying kind." Elijah clapped Phineas on the back. "Good for you. I had no idea you were in the market for a wife. How'd you find out about her?"

"She's a friend of my cousin. He lives in Texas, and we've been keeping in touch since I got here. Kind of tough with how long it takes for mail to get here, but we've been writin' all the same, and he mentioned her late last summer. I took a chance."

"I'm happy for you. I don't know anything about ranching, but I like the idea of being warm."

"I could write and see if she's got a friend."

"Oh, no!" Elijah threw up his hands as if in surrender. "I'm not looking to wed. Especially not now when I'm thinking about that possible gold in Nome, but probably not ever."

Phineas twisted his lips. "You got something against women?"

"I like my own company and only worrying about myself. I can come and go as I please, do what I want. I don't stay in one place more than a couple of years, and no woman is going to be willing to do that. They all want to settle down, build a house, and have lots of babies. That's not for me. And I have yet to meet a woman that would make me change my mind or my ways."

Chapter Two

A hot breeze fluttered the gauze curtains on the window giving no relief to the heat inside the ballroom. Tegan Llewellyn huffed out a deep sigh and plucked at the bodice of her blue silk gown. The fundraiser for the local orphanage, one of her mother's pet causes, had been going on for hours. Having started with a lecture and book reading in the late afternoon, the event continued with a four-course dinner, followed by dancing. Her cheeks ached from smiling, and her feet throbbed.

She glanced at the whirling couples, the women in a rainbow of colors. The jewels at their throats and on their wrists glittered in the gaslights. In contrast, a chamber orchestra of somber-looking men sat in the corner near the carved marble fireplace. Behind her, a trio of girls giggled and chatted, their words lost in the sound of the instruments. She probably wouldn't be interested in the conversation anyway. Most of her set were empty-headed young ladies intent on capturing a rich man so they could fill their armoires with clothes and their houses with children. Topics typically revolved around furnishings, fashion, and food, none of which held any allure for her.

With a shrug, she peeked outside at the star-filled sky. Would anyone miss her if she ducked onto the veranda to enjoy God's creation? She wouldn't be able to see much, but she could visualize the jagged range that surrounded the city. Majestic in scope and size, the mountains never ceased to take away her breath, reminding her of the Lord's omnipotence. He'd provided an adoptive family in the Llewellyns after her parents died in a house fire when she was only three years old, and He continued to supply her needs, but the emptiness in her spirit never seemed to go away. She never felt like she was truly one of them.

"You look like you've lost your best friend."

Her head shot up, and she smiled. "Wiley Caddick, where have you been? You're one of the few men who doesn't treat me like a vapid female."

"Sorry I'm late, but I got caught up in the most intriguing conversation, and the man is leaving tonight, so I had to stay."

"Stay where? What man?"

He chuckled and tweaked one of the curls dangling on the side of her face. "Should I be jealous of your interest in him?"

She swatted his arm. "Nonsense. You and I are just friends. We tried that romance thing, and it didn't end well, if you'll recall."

A shadow passed over his face, then he nodded. "I've grown up since then."

"Into a wonderful man, but not the one for me." She wrinkled her nose. "Besides, at my age that horse has left the barn. All the possible suitors my age are either betrothed or not someone I care to be saddled with for the rest of my life."

Throwing back his head, he guffawed.

Her cheeks warmed, and she pinched him. "Shh!"

"Ouch!" He grinned and rubbed his arm. "Okay, I deserved that. It was most ungentlemanly. You are a prize, Tegan. I hope you know that. And twenty-eight isn't too old to find a husband. Someday, maybe soon, a man will finally capture your heart, and I hope I'm there to see it."

"You're sweet to say that, Wiley, but I'll die a spinster, and that's not necessarily a bad thing. I like my independence."

"Are you going to commandeer all of Tegan's time?" Nolan Yates, a blond, blue-eyed giant, nudged Wiley's shoulder. "She promised me a dance, and the evening is almost over."

"Where have you been?" Wiley puffed out his chest. "I've only just arrived. In fact, you interrupted her reprimand for that very thing, and I thank you."

Tegan's heart swelled. Wiley and Nolan had been with her through thick and thin. They'd found each other on the first day of school and quickly became the three musketeers. The only misstep was during their early twenties when Wiley fancied himself in love with her. He'd finally convinced her to let him court her, and it wasn't long before she realized a marriage to him would be a disaster. Several years passed before they regained their footing as friends.

Fortunately, Wiley and Nolan both returned from the war unscathed. Eager for adventure, they'd raced to Cuba. The conflict had been brief, but bloody with the Spanish losing a significant number of soldiers there and in the Philippines. Upon returning, neither of her friends talked about their experience, remaining closemouthed when questioned.

She blinked and poked Wiley. "You were going to tell me about your *intriguing* conversation. Now that Nolan is here, you'll only have to share the story once."

Nolan's eyebrow shot up. "Do tell."

"All right." Wiley rubbed his palms together. "I was at the train station securing tickets for my parents, who are headed East to visit family, and I overheard a man telling someone that he was headed to Nome, Alaska to dig for gold."

"Gold!"

Wiley clapped his hand over her mouth. "Quiet!"

She nodded, and he removed his hand. Leaning close, she whispered. "Is there a rush? I haven't seen anything in the papers."

"He said it's only begun. He had some newspaper articles from California and Oregon. Guess they heard about it because they're on the West Coast. Anyway, he's taking the train to San Francisco, then a steamer to Nome. Reports indicate the gold is plentiful, and you can dig it up on the beach."

"You don't have to pan for it?"

He shrugged. "You can, but one article claimed that a shovelful of sand can yield several ounces of nuggets."

"Really?" Her pulse raced. Grandmother Hannah had died when Tegan was ten, but she'd read every one of the woman's diaries until she'd memorized them. Grandmother had been intrepid, staying in Georgia after her husband was murdered, to work a gold claim. To most people's shock, she'd worn pants and befriended an Indian woman. But she had lived life on her terms, unusual for a woman seventy years ago, and Tegan admired her spunk.

"Don't go getting any ideas, Tegan." Wiley frowned. "I see that look in your eye."

Hands on her hips, she glared at him. "You don't think women can be prospectors?"

"That's a loaded question. I know all about your mother and grandmother, so I have to say yes. But do you really want to go to the wilds of Alaska? You've got more riches than you could ever spend. Save the mining for men, er, folks who need the money."

"Perhaps you're right, Wiley. It'd be a long and dangerous trip, especially for a woman alone." She pinned on a smile. "Can you see my parents agreeing to such an outlandish idea?"

"Hardly."

"Now, where is that dance you promised me?" Her pulse thrummed. He'd be surprised when he discovered she'd packed her bags and slipped away to Alaska. The trip would take some planning, but she would go, and she'd be successful. Or die trying.

12

Nome, Alaska

August 1899

Chapter Three

Gulls cried overhead, their cries mingling with the shouts of the seamen on the docks. Metal clanked, and somewhere in the distance a bell rang. Tegan tightened her grip on her satchel waiting for the ramp to be lowered so she could finally disembark the cramped, churning steamer that had been her home for the last two weeks.

In comparison, the three-day train ride to San Francisco had been a picnic. She hadn't been shoulder to shoulder with perspiring, unkempt men whose leers raked her form on a regular basis. Food on the boat had been plain and filling, but hardly the kind of haute cuisine she was used to. She'd slept with her gun under her pillow, but after poking it into the stomach of the first man who tried to get *friendly*, her weapon was no longer needed. How often would she require the pistol here?

She gazed at the sky and sucked in a deep breath. Robin's-egg blue, the expanse held few clouds. The briny air was crisp and warm. Having never seen the ocean, she'd spent most of the journey on deck, amazed at the varying moods of the sea. Sometimes dark and churning, other times smooth as glass. On several occasions, fish that someone told her were called dolphins, and weren't really fish, played and swam alongside the vessel, their gray bodies glistening. As the ship got closer to Alaska, colorful birds, another passenger told her were puffins, swooped and soared ahead of them as if beckoning her toward her adventure.

Yesterday had been even more exciting when a whale had breached the surface with its tail, if that's what it was called, slapping the water and creating a massive wave. Then the creature's head appeared, and a giant stream of water had surged from a hole on its forehead. She couldn't wait to write home and describe the wonders she'd seen. How many more animals resided in the sea?

A thump sounded, and she swiveled her neck to the commotion at the far end of the deck. A pair of sailors had laid down the ramp and were securing it to the boat. Passengers pushed and shoved, jostling each other in an attempt to be the first one off the vessel. She rolled her eyes. As if thirty minutes was going to make a difference in their search for gold.

The captain barked an order, and the commotion ceased. Sheepish looks were exchanged among the travelers, and one by one they clomped down the wooden ramp onto the pier. Waiting for the last of the men to disembark, she watched the activity of the sailors as they went about their business, ignoring the passengers.

Finally free of the crowd, she picked her way across the deck, nodded to the captain, then marched off the boat. Her body swayed, and she stumbled. How odd. Despite being on solid ground, she felt as if she were still on the ocean, bucking and moving with the waves. Her heart pounded, and she pressed a hand against her thundering chest. She'd arrived. She was in Alaska. Too bad Wiley and Nolan couldn't see her now.

Tegan searched the buildings, her gaze roving the signs hanging in front of each one. First, the claims office, then the mercantile for a few supplies. She stepped forward, then was jerked back by a grip on her arm. Snarling, she yanked free. "What do you think you're doing?" She glared at her assailant, a swarthy, odiferous man of perhaps fifty. He leered at her with bleary eyes, tobacco juice staining the corners of his mouth.

"Whatcha doing here, lady? Come to show us miners a good time?" He reached for her again. She slapped away his hand, regretting that her gun was stowed in her satchel. She should have pocketed the weapon. Stupid mistake.

"Not on your life." She cradled her bag, using it to put space between her and the foul-smelling man. "I'm here for gold, just like you."

The man howled with laughter. "Well, now, ain't that a hoot. A pretty girl like you thinkin' you can last up here."

She scowled and glanced past him. Expecting help was probably unrealistic. "Look—"

"Unhand her, Stumpy." A towering giant of a man pushed his way toward them, a deep frown on his otherwise handsome face. "That's no way to treat a visitor."

Stumpy held up his arms, then cowered. "I ain't doin' nuthin', Elijah."

"Right. Why don't you go about your business?"

"I didn't mean nuthin', lady." Her assailant touched the brim of his hat, then scuttled away through the crowd.

Tegan drew her eyebrows together as she studied her rescuer. The man had to be well over six feet tall, and his broad shoulders looked as if he could carry an ox with no trouble. Crystal-blue eyes glittered at her as he removed his hat to reveal a headful of curly dark brown hair. A well-trimmed beard accentuated his square jaw. His clothes were worn but clean. Obviously, not a miner.

The man jerked his head in the direction Stumpy had disappeared. "Please tell me you've been separated by whatever man has accompanied you to Nome and that you're not here by yourself."

She straightened her spine and lifted her chin. "Not that it's any of your business, but I'm alone."

"Then you need to get back on that boat and go home. This is no place for a woman. Stumpy's harmless, but the majority of these men are not. They won't hesitate to steal your...uh...virtue, or your life."

"I'm quite capable of taking care of myself." She unbuckled her satchel and pulled out her gun. "Granted, I should have been wearing this, but now I know, and can defend myself with no problem."

"It's gonna take more than a pistol to ensure your safety, miss." He glowered. "You don't look like a *professional* girl. Why are you here?"

"To search for gold. And before you continue to lecture me about the foolishness of that decision, save your breath. I'm staying." Grandmother Hannah had more than a few entries in her diary about the prejudice she'd experienced from the men. Seventy years later, and the attitude hadn't changed. She tucked her gun into her pocket. "Thank you for your help, but I have much to do to prepare." She turned on her heel and marched toward the collection of buildings, using her satchel like a shield as she pushed her way through the mob. The man may be good-looking on the outside, but he wasn't much on the inside. One of the more arrogant men she'd met in a long time. With any luck, she wouldn't see him again.

Elijah watched the woman stomp away, her pretty face set in determination. He shook his head and huffed out a sigh. What was wrong with the people in her life who let her come to Alaska as a prospector? What were they thinking? The ratio of men to women was high, with most of the females being wives or soiled doves. Was she planning to erect a tent and live on her own? Not a good idea. She'd spend much of her time warding off unwanted advances.

Taller than most women, she had a sturdy frame, but that didn't mean she was cut out for the physicality of digging and panning for hours on end in the freezing waters of the north. His pulse increased as he thought of the shapely young woman. The dress she wore wasn't tight or inappropriate, but it did a fine job of showing off her curves. No wonder Stumpy was attracted. Every man who could draw breath would think she was a fine-looking gal. He blinked and pushed the vision out of his mind.

He couldn't pinpoint her accent, but she didn't have the long vowels of a Southern drawl or the missing Rs of a New Englander. Where was she from? Shoved from behind, he grimaced. He'd come to town for supplies, not to rescue damsels in distress, even pretty damsels, and he was staring after her like a schoolboy.

Another man tried to get friendly, and she pushed him away, her face dark. She said something to him, and the man jumped back as if poked with a branding iron. Elijah chuckled to himself. She did have spunk. He'd give her that. But she'd need more than a little gumption to survive up here. She really needed to go back where she came from.

Shoving his hat onto his head, he strode across the pier, following her to the claim's office. Hopefully, he could head her off before she wasted good money on purchasing a claim. He elbowed people aside, then stopped with a grin. She was stuck behind a line of a hundred men, perhaps more. Every passenger from her steamer was probably here to purchase or register a claim. He'd have plenty of time to convince her to leave.

"Looks like the boys beat you to the office." Elijah tucked his hands into his pockets and rocked on his heels. "Maybe there won't be a claim by the time you get to the front."

Her golden-brown eyes flashed, and she gave him a black look, erasing the fatigue he'd seen earlier. "Why are you following me?"

"Honestly, I'm not sure, but something tells me to warn you off. I'd hate to see a pretty girl like yourself get hurt, or worse."

She dropped her bag on the ground and tucked it between her feet, then crossed her arms. "Listen very closely, Mr. ...?"

"Hunter. Elijah Hunter." He cocked his head. "What's your name?"

"Tegan Llewellyn. Listen—"

"A beautiful name. You're Welsh?"

"My father is. I was born and raised in Colorado." She wagged her finger at him. "Stop distracting me. Please understand that I don't need nor am I interested in your advice. You think I'm a fool for being here. Fine. Whatever. So does my family, but I've conducted my research, and I'm old enough to know what I'm doing. And for your information, I've already purchased a claim. I'm only here to register it, then I'll be headed to the coast to do some beach mining. I'm curious as to whether the gold is as plentiful and easy to find as the newspapers say."

"Depending on where you set up, you can find a decent amount of dust and a few nuggets, but you'll need a sluice box if you don't want to break your back panning all day." What was he doing giving her advice on how to prospect as if she was going to stay? "But you still might spend more than you make."

She huffed out a loud breath. "Here's the thing. I don't need you to offer your insights on the best way to find gold. My mother and grandmother were prospecting before either of us were born. Grandmother Hannah was in Georgia during the rush of twenty-nine, and Mama worked the gold fields in Pike's Peak. Now, it's my turn. Do I think this is going to be easy? No. Do I think I can do it? Yes. So, I repeat, I'm not leaving, and nothing you say will change my mind. Are we clear?"

"As crystal." He put two fingers to the brim of his hat in salute. "Good luck to you, Miss Llewellyn. See you around." He pivoted on his heel and stalked in the direction of the mercantile. He'd wasted enough daylight on the plucky woman. Then why did he have a desire to stay and ensure her safety?

Chapter Four

Hours later, Tegan reined in her horse at the top of a berm and gazed down at the activity on the beach. She'd paid an exorbitant amount for the animal and the rest of her supplies, but she'd known that was a possibility, from Grandmother's diaries. The price of delivering her items was ludicrous but worth the extra expenditure. Would the annoying man on the pier think her naïve for her willingness to pay the outrageous amount? She blinked and shoved the thought from her mind.

Hundreds of men and a handful of women swarmed over the sand, some digging, others in the surf, still more rocking their sluice boxes. She grinned as a thrill ran up her spine. She was in Alaska.

Waves crashed onto the beach, and she inhaled deeply. The mountains were beautiful, but the sea had an allure of its own. Vast, the water stretched as far as she could see, with myriad blues and greens merging to form a kaleidoscope of color. The ever-present gulls soared overhead, their shrieks strident and loud.

The man from the mercantile drew alongside her, his cart rattling over the uneven ground. "Miss Llewellyn, where would you like your goods?"

She pointed to a space that wasn't littered with tents, far enough from the ocean so that the tide wouldn't be an issue, but close enough that she wouldn't have far to carry her items each morning.

He nodded and kneed his horse forward.

Smiling to herself, she clicked her teeth to urge her mount into following the man. She'd refused to pay the entire delivery fee upfront, and the clerk had not been happy but finally agreed. She'd also made him put the terms in writing, and a begrudging respect had glinted in his eyes. He might be able to take advantage of some of the prospectors, but she wouldn't be one of his victims.

Her horse's hooves thudded on the sandy soil as she guided him between the white tents huddled side by side. She arrived at her destination and slid from the animal's back. Casting a critical eye at the growing pile of supplies, she silently inventoried each piece. Satisfied everything she purchased had been delivered, she dug into her reticule for several coins to pay the man.

His smile flashed when he saw the amount, and he tugged at the brim of his newsboy hat. "Thank you, miss. If you need anything else, you don't hesitate to stop by the store. Nice to have someone of your caliber in Nome. Good luck to you."

"Thank *you*." She smoothed her skirts. "I'll be sure to do that." Money spoke volumes. That was the caliber to which he referred. No matter. Her initial purchases had put a larger dent in her budget than anticipated, but she'd need little from here on out. She brushed her hands together and sighed. She'd wanted to change into the pants she'd bought before coming to the beach, but the shopkeeper had been horrified at the idea of her riding through town in such a scandalous outfit. Who knew society's rules would dictate a boomtown?

"Time to get to work, girl. Enough lollygagging." Opening her reticule, she pulled out the paper on which the merchant had written the directions on how to put up the tent. Fortunately, the men were so intent on digging for riches, none of them bothered her. She set to work and within thirty minutes had the structure built. She dragged her remaining provender inside and dropped onto the trunk she also talked the man into bringing from the docks.

Her shoulders slumped as exhaustion set in. The journey had been tiring enough, but the thwarted attack on her person and the argument with the aggravating Elijah Hunter, combined with having to erect a shelter had sapped her strength. Her lips twisted, and she emitted a dry laugh. At home, she could have drawn a bath and soaked away her aches and fatigue, but those days were behind her for the near future.

Rising, she rummaged through her trunk and pulled out her boots. She wouldn't forego her dress today, but her shoes wouldn't hold up to the quagmire outside the tent. Quickly changing her footwear, she retrieved her Stetson from the luggage and clamped it on her head with a smile. Nice to be wearing remnants from home.

She marched out of the tent and squinted into the sun as she surveyed the area. Her teeth clenched. Elijah Hunter emerged from a tent nearby. How had she managed to set up camp mere yards from her adversary?

He turned and met her eyes, a frown darkening his face. To her chagrin, he began to walk toward her. Great. Another lecture from the all-knowing man. She crossed her arms and raised her chin, preparing herself for the onslaught.

"So you're really doing this?" Disdain colored his words. "Although I must admit to being impressed with your tent. Seems you're not totally without abilities."

"Stop badgering me. Don't you have gold to find?"

"I'm done for the day."

"Found your quota of riches, have you?"

"As a matter of fact—"

"Look, I don't know why you've chosen to make me your project, but I don't need your help, nor do I want it." She swept her arm wide. "I'm not moving my shelter, but there is plenty of room along the beach, so we can avoid each other. How about if we give that a try?"

A lock of hair tumbled over his forehead, and he raked his fingers through the mass of curls as he huffed out a loud breath. "You think you know what you're getting into, but hearing about prospecting isn't the same thing as doing. You might be able to handle the physical work, but you're in danger surrounded by a bunch of men who have no respect for women. You can't live alone."

Tegan clenched her fists and stuffed them into the pockets of her dress. This man's arrogance knew no bounds. "You've seen my gun. I'm quite capable of taking care of myself. And frankly, I find it hard to believe that nearly every man here plans to have his way with me and any other woman who shows up. They're too focused on making their fortune."

"You are the most hardheaded woman I've ever met," he growled. "You're—"

"Tegan!"

She turned and waved at the red-haired woman approaching on a mule. "Gretchen, you made it."

"Yes. Provisioning took longer than expected, but here I am." The young woman's face glowed. "You already have the tent up. Impressive. I would have helped."

"I know, but I was anxious to get settled." From the corner of her eye, Tegan could see Elijah gaping at Gretchen. Consternation and irritation warred for supremacy on his features, and she swallowed a grin.

Without a word, he pivoted and marched back to his tent, then went inside.

Gretchen climbed off the mule. "Did I interrupt something?"

"Only another tirade from someone who thinks he has my best interests at heart."

"Do you know him?"

Tegan shook her head. "Met him at the docks, and he's decided he's my guardian angel, although there's nothing angelic about him."

"I disagree. He's fine looking. I could get lost in those eyes of his."

"You're welcome to him. He might be handsome on the outside, but he's quite ugly on the inside. Besides, I'm not looking for a man." His image floated in her mind's eye, and she pushed it away. But if she were...

Chapter Five

Elijah's muscles bunched as he tossed another shovelful of sand into the sluice box, or rocker as some of the boys called the contraption. Whatever its name, the four-foot frame outfitted with a series of sieves was a quick way to separate the gold from dirt and gravel. He'd spent enough time hunched over a pan swirling for hours on end, but the crashing waves weren't conducive to panning anyway.

Early morning sunlight warmed his back, and he leaned on the spade's handle. Breathing deeply of the briny air, he smiled as he watched the gulls dip and dive in the sky. Their squawks and shrieks made it clear that they resented the intrusion of men into their domain. The sandpipers weren't happy, either, but lacked the courage of the gulls.

He uncapped his canteen and took a long drink, the tepid water soothing his parched throat. His gaze wandered along the coastline where men of all shapes, sizes, and nationalities worked their own boxes. A few of the miners squatted at the edge of the water with pans. Grunts mingled with thumps, bangs, and clangs as the sun continued to rise over the activity.

His take for the morning was already significant, proof of the rich veins of gold below the surface. When the mining companies got wind of the rush, they'd show up with large equipment and cheap labor, but for now the seekers were individuals, many of whom he'd seen in Canada and Cripple Creek.

Movement from the tents caught his eye, and he swiveled his neck. The Llewellyn woman and her friend each carried one end of a sluice box toward the ocean. They set it up in a small space about fifty feet away from him, in between two gnarled Californians who'd arrived a week ago.

The women jogged to their tent, then returned with shovels, pans, and gloves. He gaped as he realized they both wore denim pants, boots, and oversized shirts. Scandalous! How had they managed to secure the outfits? He barked a harsh laugh. Who was he kidding? The mercantile owner would sell anything to anyone as long as the price was right. Miss Llewellyn tucked her long honey-brown braid under her Stetson, then pulled the hat low over her face. Her partner did the same. Did they really think dressing as men would allow them to blend in to the crowds unseen? Anyone who looked at them would recognize a woman's figure.

Gritting his teeth, he continued to stare at the women. Heads close together, they seemed to be discussing something serious. Miss Llewellyn waved her hands as she spoke, her face bright and animated. The other woman, Gretchen...what was her last name...seemed to be listening intently, her eyes riveted on her friend's face. A moment later, they laughed and turned toward their equipment. The taller of the two women, by several inches, Miss Llewellyn jabbed the shovel into the sand, then swung and heaved the load into the box while her friend ensured the material fed through the riffles at a constant rate. Surprisingly, both women seemed to understand not to overfill the container.

"Nice view, but they shouldn't be here."

Elijah turned and shrugged. "I've tried to tell them that, but my words fell on deaf ears."

The miner, a lanky Scandinavian-looking man with white-blond hair and blue eyes, waved his trowel in the women's direction. "They need to leave the gold to those of us who are trying to provide for our families. This is just a lark for them."

"With any luck, they'll get discouraged and skedaddle."

"We can only hope." The man cast one final scowl at the women, then stomped away continuing to mumble to himself.

With a grin, Elijah freed his shovel from the sand and returned to work. He wasn't happy the women were here, but complaining about it didn't change the situation. The sun continued to rise. Soon it was overhead, its glaring rays heating the beach. His stomach growled, reminding him that it had been hours since breakfast. Perhaps now was as good a time as any to take a break.

He laid his tools on top of the sluice box, then took a swig from his canteen.

"Scram! You don't belong here!" An angry voice split the air followed by a woman's scream.

Elijah whipped his head around to the altercation.

A medium-built man in shabby clothes stood inches from Miss Llewellyn poking his finger at her and continuing to shout. She pushed away his hand, her mouth set in a thin slash. White-faced, Gretchen gripped the edge of the sluice box.

"Go home! This gold is for us men." The man's eyes were wide, and his skin mottled. "Cooking and having babies is all you women are good for."

Feet spread apart, Miss Llewellyn stood with her fists on her hips.

Elijah grinned. He'd seen that look, and it didn't bode well for the man who was going to get a tongue-lashing, for sure.

"I'm not going anywhere, mister, so leave me alone. I've got just as much right to be here as anyone."

"Maybe." He jabbed her shoulder, and she stumbled. A look of triumph bloomed on the man's face. "But no one wants you here."

"Don't touch me again, or I'll swear out a warrant for your arrest."

"What for?"

"Assault."

"Fine." He picked up an ax lying at his feet and swung it at the sluice box.

Gretchen leapt out of the way with a yelp, and Miss Llewellyn charged at the man as he chopped. With a grunt, she threw herself onto the culprit's back and yanked at his hair.

He screamed and threw her off, then continued hacking at the box. Shards of wood flew in every direction. She grabbed one of the larger pieces, held it like a baseball bat, and swung. The board came down on the man's back, and he hollered, then whirled.

Elijah sprinted across the wet sand. She was going to get herself killed. He grabbed Miss Llewellyn around the waist and yanked her out of the man's reach. "Stop it. Both of you."

Panting, the man ceased whacking, but the damage was already done. The box lay in pieces, the ocean nipping at the broken fragments.

She writhed and kicked like an alley cat, her shrieks rivaling that of the gulls. "Put me down. How dare you manhandle me."

"Are you crazy, woman? The man has an ax." Elijah tightened his grip. "I will not release you until you promise not to go after him. Either of you could get seriously hurt or worse. And you can't mine for gold from jail or the end of a noose."

Her lithe form went limp, and she nodded. "Fine."

He set her on her feet, then glared at the vandal. "Get out of here. You've made your point."

The man shrugged, a smirk curving his lips, then loped down the beach.

Nearby, Gretchen sobbed quietly, and Miss Llewellyn went to her, wrapping her in an embrace and sending Elijah a scathing look over the girl's shoulder.

Holding up his hands in surrender, he grimaced. He'd saved her from injury, perhaps even death, and all she could do was glare at him. He huffed out a breath and pivoted on his heel, then marched back to his box, his arms feeling strangely empty. She might be wearing a man's clothes, but the form he'd held was anything but masculine.

Chapter Six

An awkward silence hung in the air as Tegan continued to comfort Gretchen.

"You must think me a ninny." Her friend sniffled and pulled away. "Maybe I'm not cut out for this after all."

"Nonsense." Pulse slowing, Tegan squeezed her shoulder. "You're probably the smarter one of us. He made me so angry that I didn't think about what I was doing. I may be taller than most women, but if the man had a mind to, he could have hurt me badly. As much as I hate to admit it, Elijah was right. My actions were foolish."

"Are you going to get the law involved?"

Tegan rubbed the back of her neck. "I don't know. Would the sheriff actually do anything about the vandalism or subject me to another lecture on why I shouldn't be in Alaska? Two days, and all I've got to show for my efforts are a few nuggets, some gold dust, and an earful of unwanted advice." She tucked her hands into her pockets. "I'd hate to see you leave, but if you want to go—"

"I don't. This is the most fun and excitement I've ever had. I'd like to stick it out, but I thought you'd be mad that I didn't help fend off that guy."

"You had every right to be frightened." Tegan frowned. "He was wielding an ax, for goodness' sake."

Gretchen extended her arm and grinned. "Still partners?"

"Partners. No matter what." With a laugh, Tegan grasped her hand. "Care to help me clean up the mess, *partner*?"

"Absolutely."

They scooped the scraps and tangled metal into their arms, then carried them to the tent, and dumped them inside. Tegan fingered the pieces and grit her teeth. The man had done a fine job of breaking up the frame. No bigger than kindling, the wood was no good for rebuilding the sluice box.

"I'll head into town tomorrow and secure what I need to make another box. You wanna pan for the rest of the afternoon or call it quits?"

"And give that man the satisfaction of impacting our ability to mine?" Gretchen jutted out her chin, her eyes snapping. "Not on your life."

"Sounds good to me." Tegan opened her trunk, pulled out a pair of trowels and pans, and handed a set to her friend. "Daylight's burning." She exited the shelter, then marched to the shoreline, not bothering to look to the right or left. She had no interest in seeing the stares, smirks, and sneers of the miners. Grandmother's diary deserved another look. Hopefully, she included entries about dealing with the men's prejudices.

Scoop the dirt, swirl the water, tip the pan, swirl the water, pick out the gold dust. Repeat. The rhythm soothed her, and she eased out a breath. Tension seeped from her muscles. She'd let the men get under her skin, playing right into their hands. If she was going to survive this, she needed to get a handle on her emotions. Otherwise, she'd prove them right that a woman wasn't fit for mining in Alaska.

Gretchen squatted beside her and mimicked her actions, albeit with stiff and amateurish motions. "You've been here as long as me. How'd you get so proficient?"

"My folks taught us girls." Memories washed over her, and tears threatened. She swallowed past the lump that formed in her throat. "Our property had a small stream, and dad would regale us with stories of when he and Mama were part of the Pike's Peak gold rush. When we got older, we begged him to show us how." She laughed. "We were convinced we'd find great wealth in the waters behind the house."

"And did you?"

"No, but I loved the thrill of the hunt. Maybe that's why I couldn't resist coming to Nome."

"None of your sisters wanted to accompany you?"

Tegan's chest tightened as their criticisms and warnings invaded her mind. "Hardly."

"There's a lot behind that comment." Gretchen nudged her shoulder. "But we'll leave that for another discussion."

"Or not." Tegan scooped up some wet sand and grinned. Sunlight sparkled on three thimble-sized nuggets. She plucked them from the trowel, rinsed them in the water, then stuffed them into her pocket. "What do you think about seeing if any of the other women here want to join us? They might be suffering ridicule, too."

"A good idea, but they might be happy where they are."

"True. When I go into town tomorrow, I'll stop in at the claims office and ask them to inform any gals who show up that we've got room for them."

"Perfect." Gretchen wiggled her eyebrows. "Now, tell me how it felt to be grappled by that handsome man who came to your rescue."

Tegan glanced out of the corner of her eye at Elijah's tall, muscular form. Her pulse skittered, and she frowned. Better than she wanted to admit.

Waves crashed onto the sand as the tide rose. Elijah had already moved his sluice box three times since Miss Llewellyn's altercation. Perspiration slid down the sides of his face. He removed his hat and wiped at the moisture with the back of his hand, then clamped the Stetson back on. He crossed his arms and stared across the horizon.

In the distance, the glistening gray bodies of dolphins cavorted across the surface of the sea, the occasional spout of water shooting from their heads. Gulls and puffins fished with joyous abandon, their squawks and chirps triumphant. Cloudless, the cerulean sky contrasted with the turquoise, cobalt, and steel blues of the ocean.

Once again, he'd gotten so involved in digging and searching, he'd failed to take time to enjoy the view. Different than all the other places he'd been except for Dawson City, but no less beautiful. Truth be told, he preferred the mountains to the sea. The hulking majesty of the rocky and tree-covered hills always reminded him of God's power and gave him a sense of peace. Cripple Creek had been his favorite stop. To think he'd been just a few hours from Miss Llewellyn at one time.

His gaze slid to the women who were crouched at the water's edge. Heads close together, they chatted as they panned. Miss Llewellyn's motions were sure and smooth. His eyes widened. Had she participated in other rushes? An interesting thought. Gretchen's movements were awkward, and Miss Llewellyn periodically reached over to correct her.

Their backs must be aching. They'd been at the task for hours, but without a sluice box, they had little choice if they wanted to find gold. He snapped his fingers. He'd make them a replacement. They would probably reject an offer to borrow his, so he'd build them one and leave it outside their tent during the night.

As if she felt his stare, she looked over at him.

Cheeks warm at being caught mooning like a lovesick calf, he quickly turned away and busied himself with his tools. The woman had been here less than two days, and he was already getting sucked into her life. That needed to stop. Right now. Well, after he gave them the new sluice box.

"Best get to it, old man." He collected his tools, then hiked to his tent and put them inside. He grabbed a set of clean clothes and stuffed them into a saddlebag. A visit to one of the bathhouses in town wouldn't hurt. The question remained how to make the box without her knowledge. She'd know exactly what he was doing if she saw him. "I'll cross that ravine when I get there."

He ducked out of the tent and climbed the berm to where a small lean-to sheltered his horse with the few others belonging to some of the miners. He saddled the animal and swung onto its back, kneeing the gelding into action. As he rode, the tautness drained from his back, and he took in a deep breath. Much better. Being alone was easier and less stressful. Too bad he couldn't prospect without the thousands of others who'd flocked into the area. He'd have to be first for that to happen, and he was not about to trek around the country dunking his pan into every stream and river looking for gold.

The ramshackle town came into view, and he slowed the horse. A sign swinging in the breeze caught his attention: Uwe Mahr, Carpenter. No Job Too Small.

Elijah urged the horse forward, then stopped in front of the small shack that housed Mr. Mahr. He slid to the ground and tied up the animal, then knocked on the door.

"*Ja?*" The door swung open to reveal a stooped man with shaggy white hair. Sharp blue eyes peered at him through gold-rimmed spectacles. "May I help you?"

"Uh, yes, I have a rather urgent need, and I'm willing to pay extra for expedited service." Great. He'd laid all his cards on the table. He'd be overcharged for sure.

The man's eyebrows lifted, and he gestured for Elijah to step inside.

Smelling of sawdust and sweat, the room was larger than the building appeared from the outside. Projects in various stages of completion filled the surfaces. Elijah worried his lower lip. Would the man take the job, even for an enormous fee?

"What would you like me to make?"

He met Mr. Mahr's curious gaze and straightened his spine. "I need a sluice box. By tonight."

"You and everyone else." He narrowed his eyes. "Why should I put you in the front of the line?"

"I should have explained. It's for a friend."

"Uh-huh." Skepticism laced his words.

Elijah chuckled. "I'll bet you've never heard that before. This truly is for a friend, er, well, an acquaintance; she probably wouldn't call me a friend."

"A woman, eh? And she is not happy, and this sluice box will change that."

"Not if she knows it came from me." Elijah held out his hands. "One of the miners ruined hers...took an ax to it. He doesn't think the women should be here. She refuses help, so I thought you could make it and deliver it tonight or tomorrow morning. Anonymously. As I said, I'll pay extra."

"This is a generous thing you are doing." Mr. Mahr stroked his jaw. "Perhaps you will win her heart."

"Unlikely, but I'm not looking to do that. I just think we men should do right by her. I don't think she should be here, either, but to break her equipment is bad form."

"I can deliver it by six o'clock tomorrow morning. Will that suffice?"

Elijah's breath whooshed out. "That is more than sufficient. Thank you." He extracted his wallet. "How much?"

The man named a price, high but not unreasonable, and Elijah pressed several bills into his hands. He couldn't wait to see the look on Miss Llewellyn's face. She'd be angry, but thus far, the emotion had only served to make her more beautiful. He thanked Mr. Mahr, then slipped out of the shack and headed toward the bathhouse. He needed to look and smell his best for the anticipated argument with the lovely Miss Llewellyn. Whistling, he led the horse down the street.

Chapter Seven

Murky sunlight seeped through the tent walls as Tegan rolled over and stretched. Her muscles popped and complained. Between the constant light illuminating the shelter and rehashing the incident with the miner, sleep had eluded her for most of the night. She peeked over at Gretchen whose head was barely visible. She'd burrowed under the covers like a beaver in its lodge.

Tegan's stomach growled, and she cradled her midsection. When that had happened yesterday, she got up and fixed breakfast only to discover it was three o'clock in the morning. Her hand grappled on the small crate she'd set up as a nightstand for her watch, reaching, reaching. Ah, finally, her fingers wrapped around the timepiece, then she winced as the pin on its back stabbed her. She squinted at the tiny face: six o'clock. Later than she thought possible.

She swung her feet over the edge of the cot, the one item she'd splurged on. She was not going to sleep in a pile of blankets on the hard ground. Poking her feet into her boots, she grimaced at the clammy feeling that enveloped her toes. She shuffled to her trunk and pulled out a fresh shirt and undergarments. With swift motions, she changed her chemise and donned the shirt, her fingers fumbling with the buttons, then slipped into the denim pants, one of the benefits she'd quickly come to appreciate. Oh, to put her dresses behind her forever.

Rustling sounded, and she glanced at her roommate who sat up on the bed, hair sticking out in all directions. Gretchen rubbed her eyes. "Time to get up already?"

"Only if you want breakfast. I'm famished."

"What time *is* it?"

"Just after six." Tegan brushed her hair, then plaited the long strands into a thick braid. Another benefit of being outside of society. No need to primp and fuss over her appearance. She poured water from the tin pitcher into a small bowl and washed her face.

Gretchen climbed out of the cot and changed her clothes. "I'll get the fire started."

"Thanks. I'll be right there."

Her friend nodded and slipped from the tent, then popped back in. "You're going to want to see this." She held open the flap.

A shiver raced up Tegan's spine, and she stepped outside. A brand new sluice box stood next to the canvas shelter. Her head whipped up, and she searched for Elijah among the dozens of miners working along the shoreline. He wasn't in sight. Frowning, she looked at Gretchen. "You know who brought this. He had no right."

"He's being nice." Gretchen bent and ran her hand along the smooth wood. "It's beautifully constructed. The seams have been sealed. It won't leak the like other one."

"He'll want something from us."

"You read too much into this." She rose and searched the men. "But perhaps we should invite him to breakfast as a thank-you. We have plenty of food."

Tegan pinched the bridge of her nose and closed her eyes. Surely the man wanted more than a bit of food as thanks for his gift. She'd be beholden to him, and that was unacceptable. "Fine, but I'll make it clear I owe him nothing. He *chose* to replace our box. We didn't ask him to."

Gretchen knelt and began to pile small pieces of kindling. "Whatever makes you happy, but try not to be too snippy."

"Snippy?"

"Yes." Gretchen gave her a gentle smile. "I haven't known you long, but I have figured out that you like to be independent, and it sticks in your craw that someone solved a problem for you. *Without you.* Bugs you to no end." She snickered and waved toward the other tents. "Now, go and invite our new friend to breakfast."

With a flip of her hair, Tegan marched down the aisle between the shelters until she reached the one belonging to Elijah. Her heart pounded in her ears, and her mouth dried. Foolish girl. It's just a thank-you meal. She lifted her hand to knock, then swallowed a laugh. Knocking on canvas? Nonsense. "Hello? Mr. Hunter?" She cleared her throat. "Elijah?"

The flap opened a fraction, and his face appeared in the crack. "Yes? Is everything all right?"

A dark curl hung over his forehead, and she stifled the desire to brush it into place. She swallowed. "Uh, Gretchen wanted...that is, Gretchen and I wondered if you wanted to come to breakfast. The sluice box is from you, isn't it? I doubt that man who broke ours brought us one as an apology." She licked her lips. "We can pay you for the box, but she, uh, we thought you might enjoy someone else's cooking for a change."

A guarded look lurked in his eyes. "You're not mad?"

"Honestly?" She shrugged. "At first, I was, but Gretchen said something...anyway, I'm not happy you did this without asking, but it's nice to have a box. You have to tell me how much it cost, so we can repay you."

He widened the flap and came outside. "I'd love to take you up on breakfast, but I won't let you pay me back. It's a birthday gift."

She snorted a laugh. "Don't be ridiculous. My birthday was four months ago."

One eyelid lowered in a quick wink. "I'm sorry I missed it."

Her cheeks warmed, and she whirled. "Come on."

A chuckle rumbled in his chest as he followed her, and she tried to ignore the butterflies that took flight in her belly.

Casting his eyes everywhere but at Miss Llewellyn's slender form, Elijah twisted his lips. The woman was an enigma. He'd awakened and lain in his blankets waiting for her to accost him about the box. He'd imagined numerous scenarios, most of which ended with her pummeling him, sometimes with a board, other times with her fists. None of the visions included an invitation to dine.

The memory of his arms around her slim waist brought a smile to his lips. Deceptively strong, she'd been harder to control than he'd anticipated. Good thing he'd stopped her from going after the vandal. She might have actually hurt him. Or worse.

"What are you grinning at?" Miss Llewellyn stood next to the fire, a frown marring her features.

"The thought of eating a real meal. Like you said." He put two fingers to his forehead and nodded at Gretchen. "Thank you for the invitation, miss. My breakfast is normally a couple of pieces of jerky and a cup of coffee. This will be wonderful."

"You're welcome, Mr. Hunter." Gretchen beamed at him. "We appreciate your kindness at replacing our box. Cooking was the least we could do for you."

"It was my pleasure, and please call me Elijah. We're hardly in the drawing rooms of Boston."

"All right. Elijah." She motioned for him to be seated. "Did Tegan ask you the cost? We've found some gold and can reimburse you."

He lowered himself to the ground and held his hands out to the glowing wood. "No need. It seemed like the right thing to do."

Gretchen poured chunks of potatoes in the skillet nestled among the coals. "She's not going to like that, you know."

"Stop talking about me like I'm not here." Miss Llewellyn plunked down on the ground, arms folded. "We might not be in high society, but your behaviors are still rude."

Elijah swallowed a grin at the petulant tone in her voice. Her friend had a bead on her, and she knew it. Gretchen was not the simple young woman he'd surmised.

"I'm sorry, Tegan." Gretchen stirred the potatoes, and they sizzled, their starchy aroma rising about the fire. "You're right. We weren't being very nice."

"My apologies, Miss Llewellyn." Elijah's mouth watered at the heady scent of food. "But thank you for accepting my gift. I only wanted to make things right. Do I think you should be here? No. Should you and your supplies be attacked? Absolutely not, and that man was wrong."

Her skin pinked, and she rubbed at the fabric of her pants. Gretchen continued to wear a skirt. How did she feel about her friend's outrageous garments?

He took an exaggerated breath. "Who knew a lowly root vegetable could smell so good? Gretchen, you're a genius with a fry pan."

Gretchen giggled. "Not likely, but thanks for the compliment. And if I'm to call you Elijah, you must use our given names: Gretchen and

Tegan." She scooped a heaping portion of potatoes onto a tin plate, then used a wooden spoon to dig two eggs from among the smoldering embers. "Your breakfast, sir."

Warmth filled him at the woman's kindness. "Gretchen and Tegan, it is. And I'm glad to call you friends." He took the plate and set it on the ground, then tapped one of the eggs with his fork to break the shell. The women served themselves, and he began to eat. Flavor exploded on his tongue, and he moaned. Rustic fare, but tastier than anything he'd made for himself.

They ate in silence, and Elijah studied the ladies. Both were pretty, but Tegan had a beauty that outshone any woman he'd ever seen. Her high cheekbones under golden-brown eyes ringed in black and heart-shaped face were riveting. Disappearing into the collar of her shirt, her long neck was smooth and graceful. Her nose turned up slightly on the end, giving her an exotic appearance. She must be in her late twenties. Why hadn't she married yet? Were the men in Boulder blind?

"Elijah?"

"Sorry. Just woolgathering." Had they caught him staring? He glanced at his plate stunned to see that it was empty. "Delicious, Miss, er, Gretchen. Perhaps I can treat you ladies to supper sometime."

"I'd like that." Gretchen smiled. "Now, if you'll hand me your plate, I'll wash up, and we can get to mining."

He shook his head. "Let me. It's only fair." He reached for Tegan's plate, and their fingers grazed, sending a jolt all the way to his shoulder.

Chapter Eight

Fingers tingling, Elijah nearly dropped the plates. He brought up his other hand to cradle the tin dishes, then reached for Gretchen's plate. He piled everything in the iron skillet and climbed to his feet. "Anything else that needs to be washed?" Avoiding Tegan's face, he studied the collection in his arms.

"Not unless you want to do our laundry, too." Gretchen's eyes twinkled as she smirked. "I've got a couple of *things* that need to be rinsed out."

He chuckled. "You really want me to handle your unmentionables?"

She giggled. "You couldn't do any worse than my brothers."

"Your brothers did your laundry?" He cocked his head. "That must have been a sight."

"It was one of the punishments Mama would mete out when they were unruly." She nibbled her lower lip, and a shadow crossed her face. "In the beginning, they would do a poor job at it, but they learned she would make them do the task until they got it right."

"They'll make some women very happy wives."

Shaking her head, she frowned. "They were killed last year in Cuba."

Tegan gasped, and Elijah's shoulders slumped. "I'm so sorry. That must have been awful for you and your family."

Gretchen shrugged, but her hands were clenched in her lap. "They wanted adventure. They would have loved to come here and try their hand at mining. Now, they'll never have a chance." She looked up at him, tears shimmering in her eyes. "Why must men go to war, Elijah?"

"I wish I knew." He shifted on his feet. "But wars will keep happening until the good Lord returns."

Silence blanketed the air, then she swiped at her face and cleared her throat. "Ugh. I didn't mean to get so maudlin. Forgive me." She tossed sand over the fire, then scrambled to her feet. "Head to the water, and I'll join you in a moment with my laundry." She sniffled. "I promise not to bring anything embarrassing."

"For you or me?" Elijah nudged her shoulder. She was trying to put on a brave front, and he would continue the charade. "I won't peek."

A laugh burst from her lips, and relief washed over Tegan's face. She was as worried about her friend as he was. He bowed in mock seriousness. "I'll await your arrival by the ocean."

He turned and wended his way through the tent village until he arrived at the shoreline. He'd have preferred fresh water over salt to clean the dishes, but that wasn't an option. He should have put out a rain barrel, but he didn't do much cooking, and he'd heard there was little precipitation that the effort seemed wasted. The women must think him a barbarian.

Voices sounded, and he cast a glance over his shoulder. The women tromped toward him, their arms filled with clothes. The sun glinted off Tegan's honey-brown hair, and he found himself again comparing her beauty to Gretchen's. He blinked and gestured to his side. "I saved you a spot, ladies."

Tegan dropped a quick curtsy and laughed. "Thank you, kind sir."

Gretchen smiled, and she seemed to have shed her sadness. "So tell us about your family, Elijah. Do you have brothers or sisters?"

He dipped the soiled dishes in the surf. "I'm an only child, and I came late in my parents' marriage."

"They must be thrilled to have you." Tegan submerged a shirt into the water, then frowned. "Does Alaska get much rain? We should be washing in fresh water."

"Yes and no."

A wrinkle creased Tegan's forehead. "What?"

"Yes, my parents are thrilled to have me, and no, Alaska doesn't get much rain in August. We should probably haul our laundry to one of the creeks or streams around here, but with all the prospecting, I'm not sure how much room there is at the water."

"That's an interesting dilemma."

"One the newspaper articles and pamphlets failed to mention when touting why men should drop everything and hunt for gold." He rinsed the dishes and stacked them on the ground. "Whoever can figure out how to access then bottle fresh water would make a fortune. Probably more than the gold seekers."

"I'm not so sure about that. Most of these men don't seem interested in bathing or washing their clothes. I'd hazard a guess that some of the garments are so dirt-encrusted, they could stand on their own."

He threw back his head and laughed. "You may be right." Elijah continued to snicker as he glanced at her rosy face. Her expression told him that she was pleased he enjoyed her humor. His chest swelled. This was the first time she'd looked at him with genuine warmth. He was close enough to see the gold flecks in her eyes, and he found himself drowning in their caramel-colored depths. She seemed mesmerized as well, and he tore away his gaze. Focus on the task, man! "Uh, what about you, Tegan. Any siblings? And are they as tenacious and daring as you?"

"Three sisters, and I'm the youngest. They've all married and settled down." A distant look came into her eyes. "I wouldn't use either word to describe them. In fact, they think me quite mad for this *escapade*."

"Their word, not yours." He pursed his lips. "It's tough when family doesn't support your dreams, isn't it? I'm blessed that my parents let me follow my own path. They'd rather I was in a snug little cabin a stone's throw from theirs, but they understand my need to roam."

"How long have you been traveling?" Gretchen squeezed water from her skirt. "You must miss them."

"I haven't been home in…six years." The vision of his folks standing arm in arm on the porch and waving as he tromped out of sight, his satchel strapped to his back pushed its way forward in his mind. He hadn't done the math until now. How had he let so much time pass?

"What?" Tegan reared back and stared at him. "Why would you stay away that long?"

He lifted one eyebrow and gritted his teeth at the judgment in her voice. Two could play that game. "When do you plan to return home?"

"That's none of your business."

"I could say the same to you."

"Let's not argue." Gretchen held up her hands. "We were getting along. I'd like to keep it that way." She leveled a piercing look at Tegan, then swung her gaze at him, once again reminding him of her quiet strength. "Clear?"

Elijah sent them both a sheepish smile. "My apologies. Apparently, I'm feeling a bit of guilt. Even though I'll be reunited with them in heaven, they are getting older, and I'd like to see them in this lifetime."

Skepticism hovered in Tegan's eyes. "You're a believer?"

"Yes, however my outward behavior obviously needs some work since you were unaware of that fact."

"Would you be surprised to discover that I'm also a believer?"

"Um—" Stunned at the disclosure, he could hardly tell her without insulting the woman. What other information didn't he know about her?

Chapter Nine

Perspiration trickled down the sides of Tegan's face and slithered between her shoulder blades as she jammed her shovel into the wet sand. As usual, gulls shrieked at her and the other miners from above, their cries mingling with the clanks, bangs, and thumps of the gold seekers. Save for a periodic grunt or shout, conversation was nonexistent among the men. She poured the dirt into the box and exchanged a tired glance with Gretchen. Despite being active at home through horseback riding and chores around the ranch, her muscles screamed as if she normally spent her days drinking tea in the parlor.

She rotated her neck, then tried to massage away the knots, but the stiffness remained. "How are you holding up?"

Gretchen sent her a weary smile. "About as well as you, I imagine. In an odd way, I'm having the time of my life, but this is the hardest thing I've ever done." She sighed. "And today is only day five."

"We'll toughen up. I learned that riding horses, but it will take a while."

"At least I no longer have trouble sleeping. The first couple of nights were difficult with the light from a sun that barely sets. Now my eyes close almost as soon as my head hits the pillow."

"Exhaustion will do that to a girl." Tegan giggled. "Fortunately, I haven't nodded off in my dinner plate yet."

Gretchen chuckled, then sobered up. "Being here helps me understand my brothers' thirst for adventure. Not that I think war is the answer like they did, but there's something about going up against the elements that is exhilarating. Most people see a petite girl who looks like she can't lift a book, let alone do manual labor. It's been satisfying to prove them wrong."

Tegan removed her hat and fanned her face with it. "That's how I feel. Not that I'm small and cute like you, but even after only a few days, I feel better about myself. I'd like to think Grandmother Hannah would be proud of what I've done thus far."

"How long will you stay?"

"Definitely through the end of the season. I've heard they'll run us off when winter arrives. Do you know anything about that?"

"Yes, I heard a couple of the men talking. The authorities won't let anyone remain in the tent city during the frigid weather. Only folks who've built a cabin can stay."

"Makes sense. What do you think about building a place?"

"Not for me." Gretchen shook her head. "I'll head home in November. I want to be there in time for Thanksgiving. The holidays are hard without the boys, and I don't want my parents to be alone."

"You're a good daughter." Tegan's heart clenched. Would her family miss her if she didn't show up for the holidays? "What will you do after that?"

"I'd like to do something with children, but I'm not sure what. I've been praying about it, but haven't felt any sort of leading."

"Did you pray about coming to Alaska?"

"Yes."

"Really?" Tegan cocked her head, and her stomach hollowed. It had never occurred to her to include the Lord in her plans to hunt for gold. The day after hearing about the rush from Nolan, she'd packed her bags and fled Colorado, closing her ears to the naysayers. Had God sent them, or were they like Job's friends, full of their own opinions? "Well, I'm sure He'll show you the way."

"I know, but patience isn't one of my strengths." Gretchen's cheeks pinked. "I want to know now what He has in mind."

Tegan barked a laugh. "Don't we all?" She donned her hat and tugged on the brim. "I'm afraid if I go home again, I'll get sucked into the philanthropy and fundraisers of my parents. There's got to be more to life than that."

"Your parents are rich?" Gretchen lifted one eyebrow. "You said they'd been in the rush of fifty-nine, but when you didn't elaborate, I figured they hadn't done well."

"They did *very* well, as did my grandmother in twenty-nine. She and her first husband were dirt poor, and apparently, he jumped from job to job not making much money. Then he heard about the rush, and they headed into the Georgia mountains, but soon after they got there he was killed by another miner in a dispute. Grandmother decided to stay and work the claim."

"And your parents?"

"They met during the Pike's Peak rush. Mama wanted to prove herself, and they had adjoining claims. Both of them hit it big." Tegan pursed her lips. "And now it's my turn, which is why I don't understand how they could be against me."

"At their age, all they see is the danger." Gretchen stared out at the ocean. "If you didn't have to worry about what anyone said, what would you do?"

"That's a good question. I'd want to do something that makes an impact. Not like my parents giving money to a bunch of charities, but hands on, you know? Working with people who need assistance. Like the Natives here."

"What sort of help do they need?"

Tegan shrugged. "Maybe they don't need any, but I see how they're treated in town, and it doesn't seem right."

"Well, if you hide out up here, you'll never find a husband." Gretchen slid her gaze toward Elijah and winked.

"Bah!" Tegan waved her hand. "I'm not in the market. Nome men are probably no different than those in Boulder. Interested in me for my money. No thanks." And Elijah was the last man she'd consider. He couldn't stay in one place long enough to put down roots, and she wasn't going to gallivant around the country just because some man got restless.

Tegan was an heiress? Elijah's mind raced as he tossed sand in the sluice box, then rinsed the detritus through the sieves. He'd felt she was holding back when they were eating breakfast, but he never considered the fact that she might be some rich kid who was raised with the proverbial silver spoon in her mouth. No wonder she thought she could boss everyone around and be treated like royalty. She wasn't as arrogant as most people he'd met who could fund a small nation, but the money explained her poise and attitude.

Interesting that she failed to mention her financial situation. Was she ashamed of it? She probably took it for granted. Most wealthy people did. Especially those who inherited the money. What were her parents like? She'd mentioned fundraisers, but were they do-gooders hoping to be seen as generous by the public, or did they truly want to use their wealth to make a difference for the less fortunate? She was believer. Were they? What did it matter?

She was in Nome on a lark. To prove a point. She'd said so herself. He rolled his eyes, then peeked at her from under his hat. She and Gretchen had finished their conversation and gone back to work. Tegan's face was flushed, and her shirt was wet with perspiration. Her hat sat precariously on her head, and her honey-brown braid snaked down her back. She was tenacious. He'd give her that. Not like the vapid rich girls he'd seen in Cripple Creek who would have shriveled at the thought of manual labor. They used their money for fashion and fun. It sounded like Tegan was going to use hers for some sort of greater good. Or so she said.

Several small nuggets glistened at him from inside the box. He reached inside, then pocketed the chunks. A decent number of gold flakes rested in the bottom. He plucked them out with his tweezers and stowed them in the tiny screw-top vial. If he wasn't so distracted by the woman, he might find more.

A scruffy miner nearby coughed, and Elijah glanced at the man whose wolfish gaze was riveted on the women. Was the prospector simply lusting after the ladies, or had he heard their conversation? The man was close enough. Elijah surveyed the other prospectors, and a chill swept over him. Several of the men were studying Tegan and Gretchen with varying degrees of curiosity in their expressions.

Did Tegan's wealth make her more of a target than before? Not that she had hauled her bank riches with her, but would the men try to interest her as a mate? Or worse, seize her for ransom? Not that any of them appeared to be any sort of prize in their current unwashed state. How much danger lurked?

He pressed his lips together. How could she be so naïve? Reprimanding Tegan for her conversation would destroy the tentative truce they'd attained. But she needed to understand the lack of privacy and the abundance of listening ears and prying eyes. She shouldn't discuss personal information in a public place. Her tent was no better a location.

She was not in polite society where people would pretend not to have heard compromising information. Who was he kidding? Society folks might feign a lack of knowledge, but they'd use the news to their advantage.

With a loud breath, he emptied the sluice box and packed up his tools. What did he care what happened to the woman? She'd come here against the better judgment of every person she knew. She'd already been attacked once and didn't seem to think she was at any further risk. Maybe if something else did happen, she'd realize she'd made a mistake and hightail it home, back to the safety of Mama and Daddy. The sooner the better.

Chapter Ten

Tegan coughed. And coughed again. Her eyes stung, and tears streamed down her face as she sat up in bed. Across the tent, in the murky gloom, she could hear Gretchen hacking and gagging. What was happening? "Gretchen?"

She waved her arms to dispel the smoke. Smoke? She leapt from the bed and tripped over her boots, sending her to the ground.

Her roommate continued to choke and wheeze.

On her hands and knees, Tegan crawled toward the sound, the sand scraping her palms. "I'm coming." Her head bumped into the edge of Gretchen's cot, and she reached up, grappling in the air. "Where are you?"

Gretchen's hands met hers in the darkness. "Here." Cough. "Why is..." Cough. "Smoke."

"I know. We have to douse the fire."

Flames appeared at the edge of the tent in several places. Tegan's stomach clenched. How was that possible? Canvas did not readily burn. She inhaled a tentative sniff, and her nostrils burned. Alcohol. Whomever did this used liquor to start the blaze.

"Tegan!"

"Wrap your shirt over your nose and mouth, then grab your blanket, and beat at the flames. I'll do the same." She turned and tried to find her cot in the roiling darkness. Her eyes continued to weep moisture, and her throat felt as if she'd swallowed an ember. Her fingers found the bed, and she inched them along the blanket until she found her discarded shirt from the night before. She put the garment over the lower part of her face and tied the sleeves behind her head. The fabric only partially blocked the smog.

She yanked the blanket from her cot and stumbled to her feet, then made her way to the flames licking at the side of the tent. Swinging the unwieldy cover, she beat at the conflagration. Behind her, Gretchen attacked the other wall, coughing and choking as she worked.

The flame went out, but another appeared in its place. The gray smoke had turned black, and the smell of the scorched canvas was sickening. Tegan swallowed against the nausea, then winced at the pain in her throat. "Gretchen! We have to get out of here. Find the flap while I keep beating the fire."

"I've got...cough...a better...help! Someone help us," Gretchen shouted. "Help!"

"You really...think...the men are going to save...us. One of them...set this." Tegan's shoulders screamed as she continued to flail the blanket. Dizziness threatened. She swiped at her forehead with a trembling hand and held her breath. *God, where are You?*

"Tegan! Gretchen!" Elijah's voice sounded hollow as if he were in a tunnel. "Can you hear me?"

"Yes," Gretchen screamed. "We can't see."

"I'm coming."

The tent flap parted, and a shadowy figure appeared in the dreary light seeping through the opening. "This way." His arm beckoned.

Tegan's knees nearly buckled, and she staggered toward him. In front of her, Gretchen lurched toward the illumination, then faltered. Elijah wrapped one arm around her shoulder and guided her through the gap in the tent. He then reached for Tegan. She fell against him, her legs giving way. In one fluid motion, he bent and scooped her into his arms, then pushed his way through the flap.

Sweet, clean air enveloped her, and she pulled the shirt from her face to take a deep breath. Her throat seized up, and she moaned, sagging against his firm chest, his heart thumping in her ear. Steady. Comforting. Activity swirled around them as men tossed buckets of water onto the burning tent. Where had they been when the fire started? Surely, they had seen the culprit who'd done the dirty deed.

He set her on the ground next to Gretchen who hunched into herself, shoulders bowed. She gripped a tin cup in her lap. Her eyes were bloodshot and red-rimmed. Tears had tracked lines through the soot on her face. Her blonde hair was disheveled, forming a fuzzy halo around her head.

A miner she didn't recognize handed Tegan a cup filled with water, and she gulped the tepid liquid, its soothing moisture taking away some of the pain in her throat. Scrapes on her hands stung, and her chest hurt, but the outcome could have been much worse.

Elijah squatted next to the girls. "I've sent one of the men for the doc, but depending on how rowdy the town is, it could be a while before he arrives."

Gretchen nodded and sipped from her cup, her eyes downcast.

"We don't need a doctor." Tegan glared at Elijah. "We need the sheriff. This was arson, plain and simple, and someone needs to pay."

He frowned and shook his head. "You'll only antagonize the men further. We can handle this ourselves."

"What?" She narrowed her eyes. "This man needs to be punished. He could have killed us."

"I've no doubt this was another warning. Many of the miners want the women gone, and they'll do whatever it takes to frighten you." He shrugged. "The few lawmen in town have their hands full."

"So attempted murder of a woman isn't important?" She hurled the empty cup and climbed to her feet. She bit back a groan, then straightened her spine. She glared at him as he jumped up. "What kind of men think it's acceptable to kill?"

"The lawless kind." He blew out a loud breath and raked his fingers through his curls. "This isn't Boulder. This is the Wild West. Men are here to dig a fortune out of the ground and competition is fierce."

She crossed her arms and jutted out her chin. "I've got news for you. I'm not leaving."

"Well, you should." A lanky miner carrying an empty bucket appeared behind Elijah. "You being here is gonna bring nothing but trouble."

"How—"

Elijah laid a hand on his arm. "It's clear how you feel, so thanks for helping. But you know we're headed into a new century in a couple of years. Life's changing, friend, and this is just the start. Women will be doing stuff they've never done before."

The man dropped the pail on the ground, a frown etched into his face. "Fire's out, but the smoke damage is pretty bad. Don't think you can save much. Might be a good time to go home." He put two fingers to his forehead as a salute and sauntered away.

She gritted her teeth and huffed. "Why are men so bullheaded?"

"I could say the same thing about women." Elijah gave her a crooked grin. "Listen, until you ladies decide what you're going to do, you're welcome to bunk in my tent. The weather's fine. I'll sleep outside. Might deter any shenanigans."

Tegan gaped at him. First, he defended her right to be in the gold fields, then he offered her shelter. Who was this man?

Chapter Eleven

The acrid smell of smoke clung to her hair and clothes as Tegan stood and stared across the sea. Her eyes felt as if they were embedded with sand, and the image before her was blurry. Her limbs felt like lead weights, so she'd taken Elijah up on his offer to tear down the tent. After he'd finished, she and Gretchen sorted through their belongings. Fortunately, they'd discovered that other than their food and the tent, everything else could be salvaged. They'd lose a day washing every article of clothing they owned as well as their bedding, but the cots and crates they used for nightstands hadn't burned. Being metal, their cookery items had also survived.

She gritted her teeth and rubbed her hand across her forehead. Someone hated Gretchen and her enough to try to kill them. Elijah commented that it might not be personal, but just because they were women. A quick check of the undamaged tents inhabited by other female miners proved him wrong.

What had she done to make the culprit so angry? Beachfront was open and free to anyone, so she couldn't be accused of claim jumping. Was it the man who'd attacked the sluice box or one of his cronies?

Should she hunt through the prospectors for him or leave well enough alone?

"Breakfast is ready." Elijah spoke from behind her. "I owe you one after feeding me yesterday."

She turned and blinked, but his image was no clearer than that of the ocean. "We owe you for putting out the fire, and everything else." She waved a limp arm toward the tents. Her chin trembled, and she pressed her lips together.

He cocked his head. "Then you owe the boys who helped, too."

"You're right." Tegan sighed. "Do you—"

"I'm kidding. You don't owe any favors. Consider it a public service." He grinned and tugged on her arm. "Now, come eat before the food gets cold."

Another sigh escaped, and she nodded. "All right." She followed him to the campfire in front of his tent where Gretchen sat with a plate of food on her lap. She dropped to the ground, and he sat next to her, his presence bringing more comfort than she would have liked. He filled a plate with steak and fried potatoes, then handed it to her. The aroma filled her nose, and her stomach growled.

"Someone's hungry."

"Getting burned out has that effect." She sent him a smirk, then forked a potato chunk into her mouth.

"You didn't lose your sense of humor." Admiration gleamed in his eyes. "Or your appetite."

She ducked her head and continued to eat. He was just being polite. She shouldn't read anything into his look. Realizing she was wolfing down her food, she paused and glanced at Gretchen. "We need to go into town to replenish supplies and get a new tent. How soon do you want to leave?"

"I thought I'd stay and do the laundry."

Elijah cleared his throat, and the women turned toward him. "I'd rather you didn't say here alone, Gretchen. Not until we figure out who did this. I've borrowed a wagon, and if you don't mind, I'd like to tag along."

A shadow of fear marred Gretchen's features. "You make a good point."

"Thanks for the wagon, but we don't need a bodyguard." Tegan's grip tightened on her plate. "I—"

"Quit arguing. I'm low on a bunch of stuff myself. We may as well combine our trips." Elijah drank deeply from his cup. "I know you want to be independent, but sometimes efficiency takes precedence. We'll take your laundry into town, too. There's a place we can pay to wash it ourselves rather than give it to one of the laundresses."

Her face warmed, and she nodded. He'd thought of everything. She needed to stop snapping every time he made a suggestion.

Elijah gestured to the activity at the shoreline, then laced his fingers around one knee. "Your grandmother and folks would be right proud of everything you've accomplished in ten days. Few of those men took time for breakfast today, and who knows the last time they washed their clothes, but you have your priorities straight. You're eager to find gold, but the hunt is not all encompassing for you." He took her empty plate from her. "And I must admit I'm proud of you as well. You've managed to get me to change my way of thinking about you gals being here."

She gaped at him. He was proud of her? Warmth spread from her belly to the tips of her fingers and toes.

He chuckled. "I've never seen you speechless before."

Gretchen giggled. "This is definitely a first."

"Funny." Tegan tried to maintain a serious expression and failed. Laughter bubbled up. She could get used to sharing frivolity with these two. "Anyway, thanks for saying that. I hope Grandmother Hannah would be pleased. My parents..." She shrugged. "I can't reconcile who they are with the stories they used to tell. They're so..."

"Staid?" Elijah cocked his head. "Old fashioned?"

"More like proper. They're very keen about what their set thinks. Most of their friends are wealthy, and they haven't had to lift a finger their whole life. My parents worked for what they had, but it seems like they've forgotten." She hesitated, then took a deep breath. "They adopted me when I was about five years old. My real parents died in a house fire. I've never felt like one of them, although they don't treat me any differently than their own girls."

His face fell. "I'm sorry. That must have been difficult."

She plucked at her sleeve. "Some days I wonder where I belong. It wasn't Boulder, and the miners don't think it's here."

Elijah nudged Tegan's shoulder. "The woman I've met wouldn't let that stop her. She'd decide for herself." He held his breath. Would she think he was being condescending?

"You're right." Her face brightened, and she straightened. "Since when do I care what others think of me or weigh in on what I should do."

"That's my girl."

Her eyes whipped toward his, and her cheeks pinked.

"I...uh...I just mean well done," he stuttered. "I should wash the dishes."

Gretchen tittered and gave him a knowing look. "I think that's best."

Tegan busied herself with putting out the fire, her gaze studiously focusing on the job.

He turned and trudged into the tent where he had a small tub of water. Great. He'd embarrassed Tegan again. What was it about her that made him put his foot in his mouth? Regularly. On the other side of the canvas their voices murmured, but he couldn't hear the words. Probably a good thing. He hurried through the task, stacked the clean dinnerware on the small table he'd built, grabbed the women's trunk, and ducked outside.

"Is everything to be cleaned in this, ladies?" He peeked at Tegan who seemed to have recovered. Her stance was relaxed and her color normal. She sent him a timid smile.

"Yes." Gretchen clapped her hands. "Only ten days in the fields, and I'm ready for a trip to town. How silly."

"The break will do us all good." He jerked his head toward the berm. "Wagon's at the top." He tromped up the hill, the women on his heels. The sun peeked over the trees, and the tension slid from his shoulders. Since when did he look forward to errands with others, let alone two women?

They arrived at the wagon, and by the time he hefted the trunk inside, Tegan had scrambled onto the seat. Gretchen allowed him to help her up. He swallowed a smile. Some things never changed. He clambered onto the bench and grab the reins, then clicked his teeth. The wagon lurched forward, and they rode in silence for several minutes.

He glanced at Tegan, who seemed lost in thought, her eyes a distance glaze. He cleared his throat. "I've been thinking, Tegan, as believers we're adopted into God's family. Do you feel as if you don't belong?"

Her eyebrows came together, and she twisted her lips. "Hmm. I've never considered that."

"Your family chose you, like God chooses us."

"True, but did they feel compelled? Did no one else step forward?"

"Give your parents some credit. Besides, someone as cute as you? I'll bet they fell in love with you the moment they saw you."

She snorted a laugh. "You silver-tongued devil."

"At your service." His pulse thrummed, and he grinned. "Do they treat you differently? You know, did they discipline you more than your sisters? Give them gifts or show them extra kindness?"

"No, nothing like that." Tegan rubbed at her skirt. "I just feel...different. I am different. I want to try new things. They follow the rules, you know—find a husband, have a family, stay at home. That's not for me, and they don't understand." She tugged at her lower lip. "And they act as if me not wanting those things is odd."

"Did you try to help them understand?"

"What?"

"Did you ever sit down with them and try to explain your position? Explain the joy you get from exploring?"

Her gaze clouded. "No, not really. Shame on me, huh?"

"Not necessarily, if they're like my mom and dad, they want what's best for you, and they want you safe. They probably remember the dangers associated with mining. It's not that they disagree with your dreams; they're trying to keep their little girl from getting hurt. And you are their little girl, maybe not by birth, but by choice, and that makes you very special."

Understanding seemed to dawn in her eyes, and her face lit as if from within. "So, I don't have to be like my family to be part of it or to be loved. How did you get so wise?"

His chest swelled. He'd wiped away her disappointment and sadness from her expression. He could get used to doing that.

Chapter Twelve

Tools clanked and banged in the back of the wagon as Tegan rode over the uneven ground past the rows of white tents stretched along the Snake River. Looking no different than the canvas town on the beach, the area was teeming with men, horses, and equipment. A few of the miners glared at her from their locations in the water, but most were intent on panning, pulling the precious gold from the frigid waters.

On horseback, Gretchen rode beside her, with Elijah slightly behind. While leaving town yesterday, they'd seen two men burst out of one of the saloons, fighting and yelling as they rolled in the dusty street. The sight wasn't unusual, but their shouts about claim jumping and crooked judges caught Tegan's ear. Elijah had left Gretchen and her in the wagon, then sauntered into the saloon to investigate the impetus for the brawl.

It hadn't taken him long to ferret out information about Arthur Noyes, one of three judges assigned to Alaska, who regularly found in favor of claim jumpers who had little or no proof of ownership. In a case that involved one of the richest mining stakes in the district, he'd handed down an injunction and allowed the jumper to mine the claim to the exclusion of the original, and probably rightful, owner. Word had it that he was also denying owners their right to appeal.

Apparently, the scheme had been going on for a while, so after dinner the previous night Tegan came to the decision it was time to work her claim before inactivity gave anyone the idea her stake was up for grabs. Elijah agreed and announced he'd work his claim as well. When he'd laid out the map, she'd been stunned to discover their claims abutted, and a niggling thought that he was somehow involved in the nefarious ploy had dogged her most of the night.

"How much farther?" Gretchen shifted in her saddle. "And how do you know when you've arrived?"

"The wagon has been outfitted with an odometer." Tegan made a vague gesture at the bottom of the vehicle. "One of the Mormons invented it over fifty years ago. There is some sort of gear configuration that counts the miles. Only a couple more miles to go, and as we get closer, I'll check it to be sure I'm in the right place."

"Isn't that clever?"

Tegan nodded. "With nothing but trees, scrub, and water, there needs to be some method of figuring out locations."

"You got used to Boulder with its street signs and landmarks." Elijah smiled and pushed his hat back on his head.

A curl fell over his forehead, and she stifled the desire to tuck the stray lock in place. She blinked, then shook her head. They'd settled into a routine of sharing meals and digging side by side on the shore, and she was getting comfortable with him. Perhaps too comfortable. Gretchen was the only friend she needed, but he didn't seem to be going anywhere anytime soon.

She tugged on the reins. "Whoa." The wagon rolled to a stop, and she set the brake. "I think this is it, but I'll check to be sure." She climbed from the vehicle and ducked underneath to look at the cogs attached to her front wheel, then peered at the riverbank. She motioned to a vacant spot about fifty yards away and grinned. She was better at this navigation thing than she'd dared hope, proving she'd didn't need a man's help. "Just up there."

Scrambling back onto the wagon seat, she clicked her teeth and slapped the reins on the horse's rump. Moments later, she parked the conveyance between her claim and Elijah's. They erected the tents, then unloaded the supplies into the shelters. She glanced overhead at the sun, then swallowed a laugh. Of course, there was plenty of daylight remaining. The blazing ball never seemed to set.

Her stomach rumbled, and she checked the watch pinned to her shirt. Nearly two o'clock. No wonder she was hungry. She looked up as Elijah emerged from his tent carrying a skillet. Her pulse quickened. How could he look so handsome and appealing after a morning in the saddle and putting up two tents? She felt like a rumpled rag doll and had no doubt her hair was unruly despite her hat. To make matters worse, Gretchen looked fresh as a daisy.

"I'm ravenous." Elijah brushed unseen dirt from his jeans. "If one of you ladies will rustle up some biscuits, I'll build the fire and fry the potatoes and meat."

Gretchen raised her hand. "I don't have to think twice about that offer."

"I'll see about finding some firewood." Tegan headed into the trees and returned with an armload of branches. How long before the thousands of miners deforested the area? How would she start a fire for cooking if that happened?

An hour later, they sat crossed-legged in front of the glowing embers dining on the simple but filling meal. Tegan's shoulders sagged. She'd been active in Colorado but nothing like what she'd put her body through in Nome, and the rickety cot did little to comfort her aching muscles when she lay down at night. At least the trip had been successful. Only a month into her adventure, and she'd already converted the ore and dust into more than two thousand dollars.

Would her river claim prove as fruitful? Had she been foolish to give up her spot on the beach? Last night, Elijah convinced her that ownership was more important, and the longer she left her claim vacant, the higher her chances were of being jumped by one of Noyes's thugs.

She peeked at Elijah from under her bangs. He met her look with a grin, and she dropped her gaze. Gretchen snickered, and Tegan frowned. At every opportunity, her friend waffled on about the man. How he'd saved their lives and how much of a help he'd been over the weeks since their arrival.

But something about him didn't sit well. He was always at the right place at the right time. From the moment she'd stepped off the steamer, he'd been underfoot, almost as if he knew she was coming.

She froze. Had her parents made arrangements with him to talk her into leaving, and if he couldn't do that to act as a bodyguard? Was his supposed friendship merely a front for his undercover activities? Surely, Mama and Daddy wouldn't stoop to that level of subterfuge. Besides, how would they have found him? She fiddled with her braid. Maybe Elijah was part of Noyes's game and waited on the pier to watch for those who seemed to be easy pickings.

"A nugget for your thoughts." His voice broke into her musings.

"Just looking forward to the challenge of working the river. You must be, too."

He shrugged. "Panned one river, you've panned them all. I'm anxious to see how well your claim produces for you."

So he could determine whether it was worth stealing? Tegan pinned on a smile. Rather than confront him, she'd keep her suspicions to herself for a while longer.

Chapter Thirteen

The fire crackled, and sparks shot into the air, dancing on the warm breeze. Elijah poked a forkful of food into his mouth, chewing slowly. Something was bothering Tegan. He'd only known her a month, but he'd learned her tells, a skill that came in handy in the lucrative world of prospecting. Her smile was fake, and distrust clouded her eyes. What had he done or said to create the shadows on her face? And how could he find out?

Perhaps he was misreading her. The day had brought many changes as they'd moved from the beach to the river and set up camp. Was she second-guessing her decision to give up the easy pickings on the shore and work her claim in the icy waters of the Snake River?

Elijah swallowed, then took another bite of the rustic food. His gaze slid to Gretchen who surveyed their new surroundings, seemingly oblivious to her friend's shift in moods. If he were a betting man, he would have laid down money that the petite, gracious woman wouldn't have lasted a week, but she'd proven herself just as determined as Tegan. Mining was hard, physical work, but Gretchen had succeeded beyond his imagination despite her small size. She maintained a childlike innocence even in the midst of the bawdy atmosphere of the tent city, and her faith never wavered.

He couldn't say that about his own beliefs. He'd seen too much evil since leaving home. Had God's Son truly died for all men? So many seemed undeserving of His love, himself included.

"You seem to have a lot on your mind, Elijah." Gretchen cocked her head, and a slight frown creased her forehead. "Is there anything we should know about?"

"Just woolgathering." He laid his empty plate on the ground. "Although I am surprised that there doesn't seem to be as much mayhem on the river as on the beach. I guess the lack of cost to registering a claim had brought miners who might not otherwise try their hand at prospecting."

"Or maybe those who've been rooked out of their claims have packed up and gone home." Tegan rubbed her jaw. "I've been thinking about what you told us about Judge Noyes. The corruption has to reach higher. Someone else is pulling the strings on that puppet."

"You're right. I did some additional digging and discovered a political boss named McKenzie. Out of North Dakota. Even if only half the rumors are true, he's a nasty one. One guy told me the man has intimidated voters and stolen votes, and gone so far as to beat up opponents."

"And gotten away with it?" Tegan's jaw hung slack. "How is that possible?"

"With enough money, anything is possible." Elijah shrugged. "The man's greed knows no bounds, so a gold rush is right up his alley. He's probably the one who had Noyes appointed to Alaska."

"And now he's stealing claims." Her face darkened. "We have to do something about this. It's not fair."

"You can't get involved." He shook his head. "That will turn Noyes's eye onto you, and you'll lose your claim."

She clenched her fists. "But—"

"Listen, I've seen a lot in my years of making the rounds of the gold rushes. Corruption follows any enterprise that is worth large sums of money. Mining attracts the innocent and guilty alike, especially the guilty. But this scheme of Noyes's and McKenzie's is the worst I've ever seen. It involves powerful and dangerous people who will stop at nothing to feed their desire for money."

"Are you afraid?" Tegan fiddled with the seam on her pants. "Because I'm not."

"You should be." He blew out a sigh. "Treacherous men who will kill without batting an eye should be feared. But that doesn't mean I plan to sit by and let good people be swindled."

Tegan's head shot up, and her face shone. "We are going to do something."

"*We* aren't doing anything, but *I'm* going to see what I can uncover. Claim jumping has been around since the earliest rushes, but I've never seen so many ill-gotten claims get validated. I have a feeling Noyes and McKenzie are only the tip of the iceberg. This hustle probably reaches down into the claims offices and town officials. We don't know who we can trust. I need to find out how deep the rot goes."

"You have to let me do something." Her face was flushed, and her eyes blazed. "Just because I'm a woman doesn't mean I'm useless."

"I didn't say you were, but too many of us going around asking questions will draw their attention, and then we'll be dead in the water. Or just dead."

Gretchen gasped. "Tegan, you have to trust Elijah. He hasn't steered us wrong yet. In fact, he's bent over backwards to help us."

Myriad emotions played over Tegan's face, and Elijah crossed his arms. Her spunk served her well in getting her to Nome, but she was falling into stubbornness and allowing her emotions to guide her. She'd made it clear she thought she could do everything a man did, and perhaps she could, but this situation called for stealth, and that was one word he would never associate with the firebrand.

Life was easier as a loner, and he'd done fine until now. He'd avoided friendships with men, most of whom seemed shallow in their pursuit of gold to the exclusion of all else. More importantly, he'd dodged entanglements with the soiled doves and camp followers who also hoped to obtain riches by taking advantage of the lonely male population. But somehow he'd managed to get involved with the most complicated woman in Alaska, perhaps in the entire United States. How could he extricate himself? Maybe he should cut his losses and find another rush. An idea worth considering.

Chapter Fourteen

Tegan set the pan on the riverbank, then flexed her fingers. Thanks to the frigid water, she'd lost feeling in them a while ago. She shivered and stuffed her hands under her arms. The small vial tucked safely in her front pocket was nearly full, and several nuggets nestled in her shirt pocket. Not bad for a half-day's work.

She rotated her neck to ease the stiffness. Hunching over the water was going to give her a permanent stoop. She grinned. Then she'd look like the rest of the veteran miners. Proof she could keep up. But her mother would be horrified to see her youngest bent and twisted like a crone. Oh, Mama. I sure miss you. You'd love Gretchen. She's a lot like you.

Grunts, clanks, and bumps punctuated the air as the other prospectors worked. Everyone seemed to be having success. They'd apparently found a good vein. Would she hit her goal of finding ten thousand dollars' worth of the shiny ore? A drop in the proverbial bucket to her parents, but for someone who'd earned little on her own, the amount was a significant to Tegan. More than she could earn as a teacher or nurse or some other tedious job women were allowed to hold. She could do anything she wanted.

From her position on a rock in the middle of the river, Gretchen grinned at her. Eyes sparkling and cheeks flushed, she looked like a child at Christmas. Her hair was stuffed under her hat, and she wore an old skirt and blouse, but her friend was the picture of elegance. How did she do it? She was living in a tent and washing out of a bowl like Tegan. Waving, she cocked her head, a questioning expression on her face. "You all right?"

"Fine." Tegan held up her hands. "Just trying to get the blood circulating again."

Gretchen nodded, dropped her attention back to her pan, and began to hum, snatches of "Amazing Grace" drifting toward Tegan.

Lifting her chin, she gazed at the azure sky. Not a cloud marred the vibrant blue expanse. A warm breeze smelling slightly of the sea stroked her skin and rustled the strands of hair that had pulled from her braid. The green leaves and grayish-brown trunks of the trees contrasted sharply with the beige sand of the riverbed. Such a variety of color. God was amazing, and she appreciated Gretchen's reminder.

Movement to her left caught her attention, and she turned. Elijah stooped over his sluice box tinkering with one of the sieves. He'd removed his hat, and the sun shone on his dark curls. He reached for a tool, and his shirt strained against the muscles bunching in his shoulders. His long, tapered fingers wrapped around the hammer. He tapped the wire mesh in place, then rose and stowed the mallet in a leather satchel.

Her mouth dried, and her breath caught. Warmth spread from her stomach to her extremities. How as it possible that his flannel-and-denim-clad form was more handsome than any of the tuxedoed young men in her set? "Get ahold of yourself, Tegan."

She snatched up her pan and trowel, then drove the small shovel into the river bottom and dumped a pile of sand into the pan. Swirl, tip, swirl, tip. She was looking for gold, not a man. And even if she were, Elijah couldn't be trusted with her heart. He'd be on the run as soon as he got bored or heard about another rush. And he certainly didn't belong in a drawing room.

Hooves thundered, and she whirled toward the noise. A half-dozen men on horseback galloped along the river, sending clods of dirt and sand into the air behind them. Moments later, they slid from their mounts, waving papers.

Her heart clenched. Claim jumpers.

Tall and bearded, the man in front approached her while his companions sought out other miners.

She climbed to her feet and put her fists on her hips. Scowling, she remained mute. She wouldn't give him any ammunition by speaking first.

Unlike the others who whooped and hollered like banshees, the man touched the brim of his hat, then dipped his head in greeting. "Good afternoon, miss. My name is Jake Johnston, and I'm afraid you're on my land. This is my claim." He held out a folded sheet of paper. "This will explain everything."

"You're a fraud." Moisture sprang out on her palms, and perspiration trickled down her spine, but she wouldn't show him her fear. She flicked her gaze at the page, then back to his face. "I own my claim, and it's registered. You and your friends need to clear out."

His face darkened. "You're mistaken, little lady. This has been signed by a judge, and what he says goes."

"And depending on the judge's name, that signature isn't worth the ink used to write it."

"No!" A gunshot rang out, and she jerked her eyes toward the commotion. One of the claim jumpers lay on the ground, gripping his arm and writhing in pain. A miner stood over him, gun clenched in his hand. Elijah also held a gun at one of the jumpers. The situation was disintegrating.

Johnston threw the paper on the ground at her feet, then raced toward his accomplice and knelt beside the injured man. He shouted at the miner, "If he dies, I'll see you hanging on the end of a rope."

"Not before I see you in jail for trying to steal what's mine." The prospector looked mulish and not the least bit frightened by the man's threat. "Now, get that worthless piece of trash off *my* property."

"I suggest you do as he says, Kendrick." Elijah pulled back the hammer on his weapon. "And Seager's only got a flesh wound, but a trip to the doc wouldn't be a bad idea."

Tegan gaped at Elijah. He'd called the men by name. Did he know them? Was his familiarity with them further proof he was part of the chicanery?

Head close to the miner, Elijah said a few words she didn't catch. The shooter tucked his pistol into the waistband and nodded, then responded. They continued to talk for a few more minutes, and she stifled the desire to move closer so she could hear. A touch on her arm made her jump.

White-faced, Gretchen stood next to her. At some point, she'd made her way to the shore.

Tegan grimaced. She'd been so engrossed in the incident, she hadn't given her roommate a single thought. What kind of friend was she?

Elijah glanced toward her, then pivoted and hurried toward his tent. What was he up to?

Chapter Fifteen

"Hello?"

Tegan froze, one foot hovering above her boot. She hadn't seen Elijah since yesterday when he'd disappeared on the heels of the claim jumpers. Last night, she'd loitered in front of the campfire outside her tent until she'd nearly nodded off into the flames, yet he hadn't returned to his shelter.

"Just a moment." She jammed her foot into the boot, then fumbled with the laces. Good grief. How could the sound of his rumbling voice turn her into Nervous Nellie? She grabbed the brush from the crate she used as a nightstand, raked the tangles from her hair, then braided the tresses into a single plait. She smoothed her hands down her shirt and pants. Rolling her eyes, she snatched her hat from the bed and shoved it onto her head.

She pushed aside the flap and stepped outside, squinting against the glare. Seven o'clock, and the sun was already shining as if it was noon. She glanced at Gretchen who stirred a pot of oats over the embers. Her stomach growled at the nutty, slightly sweet scent.

Hat clenched in one hand, he raked his fingers through his riot of dark curls. "Sorry if I woke you."

"Nah." Tegan took the mug of oatmeal Gretchen was holding out for her. "I was already up but getting a slow start. I'm not so driven by gold fever to work twelve hours a day. I'm fortunate that my claim has been producing." She cocked her head. "You raced out of here after the jumpers, so I hope you bring news."

"Yep. I followed them, and they're staying in one of the seedier boarding houses."

"You called one by name." She narrowed her eyes and let the words hang in the air.

"What are you trying to say?" Face flushed, he crossed his arms, hat dangling from his fingers. "You're usually more direct with your accusations."

"There are thousands of men here. I find it suspicious that you were able to identify one of the jumpers. I never see you go into town, so it's not like you're hanging out at the saloons or cat houses. How would you know the man?"

"We're well acquainted. Kendrick has been trying to take advantage of people since he arrived, and I was one of his first targets. I found him in my tent, stealing stuff from my trunk. I bested him in the tussle and dragged him to see the sheriff. Unfortunately, there were more serious crimes to be prosecuted, and he was let go with a warning to keep his sticky hands to himself. Seems like he's decided to up his game."

"A warning?" Gretchen frowned. "Hardly seems fair."

"Unfortunately, since he never actually got away with any of my stuff, the law wasn't interested in attempted theft."

Tegan tugged at her braid. "How'd you come by a claim right next to mine?"

He held up his hands as if in surrender. "That was pure happenstance. Truly." A smile curved one side of his mouth. "Although I must admit, I was pleased at the coincidence. I didn't come to Nome looking for friends, but I've enjoyed you ladies' companionship."

"And we've enjoyed yours." Gretchen beamed at Elijah. "Haven't we, Tegan?"

"Sure."

"I'm not convinced." Elijah winked at her. "I wasn't hiding anything. Honest. The topic of our river claims only came up recently. Frankly, I'd rather work the beach because it's easier, and I certainly don't have to worry about jumpers, but I own this stake fair and square, so, like you, I figured I better work it. And it's a good thing, too. Otherwise, I wouldn't have been here when those guys showed up to take it."

"I think they waited until we were here. They could have already been working our claims, but they came the day after we did. That's no accident." She clenched her fists. "They have the judge on their side, so they pretend to go through due process."

"I plan to go through the real process." He rocked on his heels. "That's what I came over to say. I'm headed to San Francisco. The Ninth Circuit Court of Appeals is down there."

Disappointment hollowed Tegan's belly. He was leaving. "That's the closest place?"

"Yep." He plunked his hat on his head, then reached into his shirt pocket and pulled out a folded sheaf of papers. "Since we don't know how far the corruption goes, it's best if I leave the area to get this taken care of. Sending a telegram won't show them the proof, and I can't be guaranteed the cable will be sent. I can speak on your behalf, if you give me power of attorney. I've already got permission from a couple of others who've been scammed out of their stakes."

She scowled. "I thought you knew me better than that. What in our history makes you think I'd give you, a man, power of attorney? I'm capable of speaking on my own behalf, and I've still got the paperwork they threw at me."

Fanning the bundle, he lifted one shoulder. "Suit yourself, but you're gonna want to stick with me. Noyes was foolish enough to keep copies of a couple of letters he sent to his boss about this scheme. And I've got them."

"You *stole* from these guys?"

Triumph gleamed in his eyes, and he nodded. "You'd think they'd do a better job of safekeeping their deeds, but the papers were in a drawer in his unlocked desk. Not too bright."

"But you stole them."

"Do you have a problem with that?"

She wrung her hands. "I don't know. Do two wrongs make a right? Doesn't stealing to prove our point make us no better than these men? Technically, you broke the law. What if the courts find you guilty of that?"

Hesitation danced across his face. "I'll cross that river when I get there, and if you're not comfortable with me standing in for you or heading down yourself, then be prepared to lose your claim."

A chill swept over her. Whether or not she liked it, he was right. She had to do something to prove the claim was hers. The men had been run off, but they'd be back, and probably sooner than she'd like. But to hand over her legal rights to Elijah? No matter how much she'd grown to like and even respect him, she wasn't about to give him power of attorney. Nope. She'd head to San Francisco with him. Her pulse skittered. To spend two weeks on a steamer with the man? What would that be like?

"I see the resignation on your face. What did you decide?"

Chapter Sixteen

A deep frown wrinkled Tegan's forehead, and Elijah waited while she seemed to continue arguing with herself. Alternately trusting and suspicious, she was an enigma. Of course, all women were a mystery to him, his mother included. Why had she been willing to follow his father's endless pursuit of dreams that never came to fruition? Did she love him that much?

He clamped his lips together. He'd made his case. The decision was hers, and he wouldn't beg her to go or caution her to stay. He doubted anything he said would influence her. She'd either let him act on her behalf or not.

With a shrug, he stuffed the sheaf of papers into his pocket, then reached toward the coffeepot nestled in the embers. Gretchen handed him a cup and rolled her eyes, a tiny smile tugging at the corner of her lips. She was a sweet woman. Why couldn't he be drawn to someone like her rather than the bullheaded Tegan?

His back to Tegan, he squatted next to the fire and sipped the dark brew. "How do you manage to make such good coffee?"

Gretchen grinned, her cheeks tinged with pink. "Patience, of which you have little."

Elijah roared with laughter. "You've grown to know me quite well. At least you're willing to share."

"When do we leave?" Tegan's voice was tentative, unusual for the strong-willed woman. "I need time to make arrangements."

He drained the last of the drink, then wiped his lips with the back of his hand before climbing to his feet. "Make them quickly. There's a steamer leaving in the morning, and I plan to be on it."

A gust of wind ruffled her bangs and pulled loose a lock of hair. He stifled the desire to tuck the silky lock behind her ear. "The boat pushes off just after dawn."

She caught her lower lip between her teeth and gave him a curt nod. "So be it." Her glance cut toward Gretchen. "Will you come with us? You won't be safe here on your own."

"Unless you want me to work your claim until you return, I plan to head back to the beach."

"That would be safer." Tegan rocked on her heels. "Not to tell you what to do, but—"

"I'll make arrangements to bunk with some of the women, so you can quit worrying about me." Gretchen spread the embers, then sprinkled dirt over the glow until a tiny curl of smoke indicated the fire was out. She pierced Elijah with her gaze. "Take care of her. I don't want to see her get hurt."

"Aye, capt'n." Elijah put two fingers to the brim of his hat. "Any other orders." Her eyes narrowed further, and he straightened. Was she referring to the boat ride, the appeal, or something else...perhaps him. "I won't let anything happen to her."

"See that you don't."

Tegan waved her hands. "Hello. I'm right here. Do you have to talk about me like I'm not?"

Gretchen rose and buffed Tegan's shoulder. "Sorry. My brother always said I smothered him. Guess I haven't broken the habit."

"No, it's me who's sorry. I overreacted." Tegan squeezed Gretchen's arm. "It's nice to have a friend looking after me."

Stomach clenching, Elijah dug the toe of his boot into the ground. After all he'd done to help her, and did she not consider him a friend? What did she think of their relationship? Could he use that word to describe what they had? What did they have? The trip to San Francisco yawned. Two weeks on a steamer with her. How would that affect things?

"You have two." Gretchen jabbed Tegan with her elbow. "Elijah didn't have to come and offer to represent you or tell you of his plans."

Face pale, Tegan stared at his chin and mumbled, "You're right. I appreciate all you've done. I'm grateful." Her voice was wooden, and she sounded anything but appreciative.

Shouts and laughter floated toward them from the river, and they turned to watch a trio of men slap each other on the back. One of the miners reached into his pan and held up a nugget the size of an egg. Elijah pursed his lips. No wonder the men were celebrating. However, broadcasting their find was a dangerous move. How many of the prospectors would be willing to kill to get their hands on a piece of gold that large?

The men's shenanigans seemed to break Tegan's mood. The lines smoothed from her face, and her movements as she collected the soiled dishes were relaxed. "I'll wash up, then head to town to purchase my ticket..." Her eyebrow lifted, and she looked at him, her head cocked. "Unless you've already done so."

"Guilty as charged." His pulse raced as he waited for the anger that was sure to come, then grinned when Gretchen coughed to cover a giggle. She knew her friend wouldn't be happy with his actions but was obviously amused that he'd taken the risk. Although it hadn't been much of a danger. He knew she wouldn't give him control of her affairs. A trip with him to San Francisco would be the lesser of two evils. "I figured I could always sell it to someone else or return it. I didn't want you to lose a spot."

"Are there that many people heading out?"

"I didn't want to take a chance."

"Thanks." Her eyes sparkled, and she actually sounded like she appreciated his gesture this time. "Makes sense."

He pushed his hat away from his forehead. "You're not mad?"

"I should be." She shot him a dazzling smile. "But you've saved me some time. Now we can get Gretchen settled at the beach."

His breath came out in a whoosh. He would never understand the woman. One minute she seemed ready to wallop him, and the next she was looking at him as if he'd granted her wildest dream. The result was that he went from being irritated at her and wishing she'd never entered his life to a powerful desire to pull her into his arms protecting her from all danger. Unable to think of how to respond, he cleared his throat and nodded. Yes, it was going to be a long voyage.

Chapter Seventeen

Black smoke puffed from the stack in the middle of the boat as Tegan clung to the rail. The ocean churned, and waves buffeted the sides of the vessel. Gusts of wind wrestled with her skirt, and she began to rue the decision to wear a dress after so many weeks of jeans. Not that she'd had any choice. No decent woman wore pants in public. She could get away with it in the wild gold fields of Nome, but not in polite society.

Three days had passed since they pulled away from the docks, and the passengers had settled into a routine after learning how to stay out of the sailors' way. It had taken two days for her to get her sea legs. She no longer staggered on the decks like a drunk or lost her footing on the stairs to the hold where her cabin resided.

Another gust of wind tugged at her skirts, and she tightened her grip on the rail, its wood smooth against her palm. Except for an occasional breach of the water's surface, the whales remained underwater. Smarter than she was, no doubt, but the idea of being sequestered in the tiny airless cabin held no allure.

Small and dark, the room had four bunks and barely enough space to store the inhabitants' trunks. Another reason to deplore the fact she needed a large piece of luggage to store her dresses. In an effort to cram as many souls on his boat as possible, the captain assigned the wives of the three married couples who were leaving to her cabin. Their husbands bunked with the single men. The women hadn't been happy about the arrangements, but the man had remained firm.

She rarely saw the wives who fled their accommodations early each morning and didn't return until well after dinner. Was it that important for them to spend all day with their husbands? Didn't they want time to themselves? As anticipated, they'd seemed shocked, then disdainful when she revealed that she was unmarried yet traveling with Elijah. The new century was looming, yet the same provincial attitudes pervaded, even in Alaska. When would a woman be allowed to move freely?

Unlike Elijah who prowled the decks on his own, often trying to cajole the deckhands into letting him help with the chores. The captain had finally allowed him to assist after Elijah assured him that he wasn't looking for a free or reduced-cost ride to San Francisco.

Movement caught her eye, and she turned to see him swabbing the decks. Despite the chill, he'd shucked his coat. His muscles bunched and rippled under his flannel shirt, and the breeze ruffled his curls. Seemingly unaware of his surroundings, he leaned into his work, mouth set in a thin line, gaze riveted on the mop he pushed back and forth. The man did nothing halfway. Even cleaning the deck took all his attention as if he were preparing a ballroom floor.

His sleeves were rolled up, revealing his corded forearms. Tanned from being outside since May, his skin glowed golden brown. A tuft of black hair peeked out from where his shirt was unbuttoned at the neck.

Her mouth dried, and her pulse quickened. How could he annoy and attract her at the same time? She pounded the rail. Standing here mooning was a waste of time. Surely, there was something she could do to pass the hours.

He looked up and grinned, then leaned his mop against the wall. If that's what it was called. She'd learned on her last trip that the front of the ship was the bow, the back was the stern. Left was port and right was starboard. Who'd dreamed up those terms that made no sense at all? Traveling by boat was necessary on this journey, but she preferred a train any day of the week.

"A nugget for your thoughts." He wiped the beads of perspiration from his forehead with his sleeve, then gestured to the water. "Enjoying the view?"

"Gorgeous, but chilly." She returned his smile, and her belly warmed. Focus, girl! "The sailors must be happy to have your assistance."

With a shrug, he glanced over his shoulder. "I'm not sure how happy they are, but the tasks give me something to do. You must be bored."

"Terribly. Even though this is a passenger ship, the captain has done little to cater to his guests. I was hoping for at least a small library, but that appears to be too much to ask for."

A chuckle rumbled in his chest. "He's carting miners back and forth between Nome and Alaska. Hardly the clientele that would be looking for literary pursuits."

She giggled, then pressed her lips together. Since when did she giggle? "True." She cleared her throat, then ducked her head. "Thanks for letting me tag along. I could have handled this on my own, but it's nice to have a partner."

"Anytime." With a gentle touch, he raised her chin with his finger, then winked when she met his eyes. "Partner."

Her heart threatened to jump from her chest as his gaze seemed to caress her face. He lowered his hand, but she could still feel his touch on her skin. What was wrong with her? She wasn't looking for a husband, and even if she was, Elijah couldn't possibly be a candidate. At some point, he'd get tired of being in Nome and head to the next rush, whether gold, silver, or copper. Or some other ore that had yet to be discovered. He was an adventurer, not a homebody. He was not a man to settle down and raise a family.

Tegan licked her lips, and his gaze shot to her mouth. Her surroundings faded away, and time froze as he bent his head. His face came close, and his eyes searched hers, probing the depths. Trembling, she inched forward until she was a breath away. His lips came down on hers, soft at first, then more firm. He pulled her toward him, and she slid her arms around his neck, drinking in the taste of him. So much for remaining aloof.

Chapter Eighteen

Elijah's scalp tingled as Tegan threaded her fingers through his hair. Her lips were warm and soft on his, her lithe form molded against him. The steamer lurched, breaking their connection. Her eyes popped open, and she jerked away from him. Face flushed, she wrapped her arms around her midsection as her color heightened.

"How dare you take liberties with me!" She gestured around them. "Especially in public. Do you care nothing for my reputation? Just because we're friends, and I agreed to travel without a chaperone doesn't give you the right to kiss me."

His cheeks scorched at her accusation, but he stiffened his spine. Putting his fists on his hips, he frowned. "That's not what...I mean...it just sort of happened." He sighed. What had he been thinking to kiss her? He hadn't been thinking. That was the problem. He'd allowed her beauty to overwhelm him, and he'd dropped the wall around his heart, letting her in. And now his actions had ruined what they had. "I'm not the kind of man to take advantage of a lady. I...uh...got caught up. It won't happen again."

"See that it doesn't." She glared at him. "I can't believe you kissed me."

He was tired of being reprimanded. "You responded."

"What?"

"You responded to the kiss. It was not one sided, so you might give that some thought while you're hollering at me. Blaming me."

"How dare you." She pulled herself to her full height, but she still stood inches shorter than him.

"How dare I state the truth? Dare to say that you liked the kiss no matter how much you're sputtering and spitting now?" He enjoyed the uncertainty that clouded her expression. Perhaps he enjoyed her discomfort more than he should. "Maybe you're not as upset as you pretend, or mad at yourself for liking it. Do you have feelings you don't want to admit?" He clamped his lips together. He'd probably gone too far with that one.

She poked his chest with her finger. "Of all the arrogant things to say. You think you're such a prize? That every woman you meet, including me, is attracted to you? That we'll fall on our knees, thanking our lucky stars that you've deigned to notice us and grant us your affections? Well, you're wrong. You can't stay in one place longer than it takes to play out the gold or be bothered to take on responsibilities. What woman wants a man like that? Stay away from me. I don't want to see you again until we get to San Francisco, then we'll deal with the fraud together only because we have to."

Stomach curdling, he nodded. She whirled and stomped away, the heels of her boots striking the deck like a hammer on an anvil. He watched her for a long moment, then shook his head and trudged back to where he'd left the mop and bucket. He was a fool, and it was his own fault. He'd gotten involved the moment she set foot on the docks in Nome when he told her to leave. That should have been the end of things, but instead he'd continued to dog her with unwanted advice until he'd decided she couldn't manage without him.

Tegan was right. He was arrogant. He raked his fingers through his hair, then grabbed the mop handle and attacked the deck with a vengeance.

"Women are difficult to understand, aren't they?"

Elijah whipped up his head.

Arms crossed, one of the sailors, a grizzled man of indeterminate age smirked at him. "But with a little prayer and sensitivity, she'll come around."

"Hardly." Elijah barked a laugh. "And she's right. What woman would want me?"

The man held out his hand. "The name's Mac, and you're Elijah, right? You've done us a great service by helping out."

Elijah shrugged. "Beats lollygagging at the rail."

"Nonsense. I've been sailing a lot of years, and you're the first passenger to lend a hand. Says something about you, lad. I've watched you. You're a good man, full of integrity."

Another shrug. "No better than anyone else."

"None of us is." Mac squinted at him. "Why are you and that little lady headed to Frisco? Tired of digging for gold?"

"No, we're going to the court of appeals to get validation of our claims. Corruption is running deep in Nome, and we aim to do something about it. Jumpers are stealing claims right and left, and the local judge is signing off on their paperwork. The original claim holders are being robbed."

"See, I knew you were an honorable man. Righting the wrongs happening up north." Mac stroked his jaw. "I'll add that to my prayer list. And not that it's my business, but I'll talk to the good Lord about your romance troubles, too."

"You're a believer?" Elijah cocked his head. "How's that sit with the other sailors?"

The man chuckled. "Not always too good, if you can imagine, but they've learned I don't judge them. Sometimes they actually ask me about God, and we talk. No one's taken the plunge yet, but maybe I'm just here to plant the seeds." Mac smiled. "Seems like you might be a believer."

"Yes, but I stumble a lot. I'm not sure the miners know."

"We all make mistakes, lad. Our response to them is what's important, and you might be surprised at how many of them sense something's different about you. Maybe when you get back, you can figure out a way to let them know what it is."

"I'm not a missionary."

"We're all missionaries whether we want to be or not." Mac squeezed Elijah's shoulder. "Now, it's back to work for both us of before the captain catches sight of us jawing. Remember, I'll be praying for you and the lady."

"There's nothing to pray about."

"Yeah, there is. You just don't know it yet." With a wink, the man turned and sauntered off, hands stuffed in his pockets.

Elijah swirled the mop in the bucket, then thunked it onto the deck and began to scrub. Did he want things to work out with Tegan? It would take a miracle to make it happen.

Chapter Nineteen

Another day staring across the cobalt-blue waters as the steamer made its way to San Francisco. Another day of solitude among the passengers. Tegan pressed her lips together and gripped the railing as a gust of wind pushed against her. Her skirts whipped around her legs, and tendrils of hair escaped the braid that hung down her back. She squinted into the sun and searched the churning ocean for signs of sea life. Anything to break up the monotony.

Over a week had passed since her argument with Elijah, and she'd only caught sight of him twice. Each time, he'd ducked his head, averted his gaze, and hurried away. She didn't blame him. What man would want to spend time with a shrew? Besides, she'd made it clear she wanted him to stay away.

She rubbed at a worn spot on the wooden rail and worried her lower lip. He'd done what she'd asked, and within minutes she regretted her words. But pride refused to let her seek him out to apologize. She felt his absence keenly. She'd gotten used to having him around. No, it was more than that. She'd responded to his kiss because she felt something. Something deep within her. And now it was too late. Even if he wasn't hurt by her accusations, he wouldn't want to be friends, let alone anything more. Not after all the ugliness she'd thrown at him.

How could she have judged Elijah and found him lacking? Just because he moved regularly to follow the rushes didn't mean he was irresponsible. She'd never seen him drink, and his trips into the boomtown were during the day and long enough to collect supplies, obviously not throwing his money away on the vices available to the prospectors. He'd been respectful to her and Gretchen.

Tegan raised her gaze to the cloudless blue sky. *Forgive me, Lord. I've been prideful and mean. Not the kind of witness to others You would have me be. And I've torn down a fellow believer. The verse in James about the tongue being full of deadly poison is true. Cleanse me, Father. And if You're so inclined, please provide an opportunity to make things right.*

Footsteps sounded behind her, and she flinched. God hadn't wasted any time in answering her prayer. She recognized Elijah's tread. Dare she look at him? Her pulse skittered, and her mouth dried. Cowardice wasn't like her, but then no man had ever affected her like the tall, broad-shouldered miner.

"Tegan?" His voice was warm, yet tentative. He was probably waiting for her to hurl more venom at him.

She pivoted and smoothed her skirts. "Yes?"

Sunlight glistened on his curls, and his crystal-blue eyes sparkled against his tanned face. "Listen, I know you told me to stay away, and I'll leave you alone in a minute, but I wanted to say I'm real sorry about what happened. You have every right to be angry with me. Anyway, that's all, and now I'll—"

"Wait." She grabbed his arm, then pulled back as if scalded, but her palm tingled from the warmth of his skin. "Don't go. I wanted to apologize, too." She barked a dry laugh. "In fact, I just prayed asking for the chance to do so, and here you are." She stuffed her hands into the pockets of her skirts to quell the desire to take his hand or worse, pull him toward her. "I overreacted and said some horrible things. Can you forgive me?"

His teeth flashed as he shot her a bright smile that lit up his face. "Nothing to forgive. It's all my fault. Your reaction is totally understandable. I broke your trust by kissing you. We had a good thing going with our friendship, and I almost ruined that." He winked. "Of course, if you weren't so beautiful, smart, and fun, I might not have been tempted."

Her cheeks burned, and she shook her head. He was trying to make her feel better, but his words sent a thrill up her back. He couldn't possibly be attracted to her. She was unfeminine, difficult, and opinionated. But it was nice to hear the compliments.

Even if he was interested, he wasn't here for the long haul. He'd head out as soon as he heard about the next rush. And the last thing he'd want was her tagging along. Her stomach hollowed at the thought.

Elijah reached toward Tegan to lift her chin, so she'd look him in the eye, but dropped his hand. That move was what started the problem in the first place. And if he touched her, he couldn't count on behaving himself. Not after he knew what it was like to kiss her and feel her melt against him. No matter what she said, her response told him she felt something. Hopefully, it wasn't simple loneliness.

He cleared his throat. "Can we call a truce? Start over?"

With a saucy grin, she said, "You mean like to the beginning when you told me to go back where I came from?"

"I was awful, wasn't I?" He tilted his head. "No, to the part where you, Gretchen, and I shared meals."

"Perfect." Her smile was dazzling. "You've got yourself a deal, friend."

Tearing his gaze away from her mouth, he nodded as his heart clenched. She'd called him friend. Would she ever want more? "We won't discuss what happened ever again. A clean slate it is." He gestured toward the bow. "Would you care for a turn around the deck, *friend*?"

A giggle escaped, reminding him of the silver bells he'd once heard. "That would be delightful."

He chuckled at their mock formality and crooked his elbow so she could take his arm. When she slid her hand in the hollow, a *zing* shot to his shoulder, and his eyes widened. Had she felt that, too? Stop it, man.

You've a task to complete, and she made it clear that friendship is all she wants.

They sauntered along the wooden boards, evading the crewmen. When they passed Mac, he glanced at them and saluted, his eyes twinkling and a broad grin on his face. Elijah swallowed a laugh. The old codger had obviously worked overtime in his prayer life and was pleased to see Tegan on his arm. He'd chase down the man later and tell him how things had worked out. He acknowledged him with a nod, then turned his attention back to the woman with the golden-brown eyes. He forced himself to think about the reason for their journey rather than noting how the sun brought out the red and gold highlights in her hair. "We should arrive in San Francisco in another couple of days."

"Good. I'm anxious to get our claims validated so we can return to Nome. I hate being away for so long."

"Me too, but I don't know how long it will take for us to get on the docket. Could be days or even weeks."

"Weeks?" She pressed one hand against her throat. "That would be terrible."

"Agreed." He patted her hand. "But as hard as it is to remember, God's in control, and he'll handle this for us. He knows what we need and has already gone ahead of us to work out the situation."

"You're right." Her mouth twisted into a wry smile. "I'm running ahead of Him again. Happens too often."

"Trust me when I say you're not alone in that. I do it all the time." His stomach rumbled, and he pressed his free hand against his middle. "Apparently, I'm hungry. Let's head to the galley and see how close they are to having dinner ready."

A gong sounded, and Tegan nudged his shoulder. "Your timing is impeccable."

"I'm afraid I can't say the same about our meal."

"The food hasn't been that bad. A tad simple perhaps, but filling and plentiful."

"True." Elijah led her below deck, and they made their way to the dining area. Several passengers had already arrived, but there was still room at the long plank tables that filled the room. "Let me get you seated, then I'll grab our food."

She beamed at him, and his chest swelled as he helped her thread her way through the benches to a vacant place near one of the portholes. After he seated her, he hurried back to the spot where the cook was filling plates with steaming fried potatoes and fish. Again. They'd eaten their weight in fish, but at least it was fresh, and he didn't have to worry about food poisoning. He carried the dishes to the table and bowed as he set down the plates. "Your dinner, madam."

"It looks divine." She bestowed another brilliant smile on him.

Lowering himself onto the bench next to her, he caught a whiff of her crisp soapy scent. How did she remain so clean in cramped quarters? "Not really, but I'm sure the *chef* appreciates your assessment."

Tegan snickered, then bowed her head. Her lips moved silently as she prayed.

He tore away his gaze and closed his eyes. He should thank God for healing their friendship, but he wanted more, and wanting more and getting more were two different things. He was nothing like the man she deserved.

Chapter Twenty

Elijah shouldered his way down the sidewalk. He hated cities, and San Francisco was the largest he'd been in. One of the crewmen on the steamer said there were nearly three hundred and fifty thousand residents. The gold rush in forty-nine had started the growth, but about twenty-five years ago the population had exploded. He shuddered and hunched into himself. Way too much humanity for his taste.

He peeked at Tegan who walked by his side. She didn't seem as bothered by the crowds. Instead, she looked around as she walked, seeming to take the noise and chaos in stride. They'd arrived two days ago and experienced nothing but frustration and setbacks since setting foot on soil.

The sun was heading toward the horizon, the blazing ball's gold and orange rays casting shadows on the streets. One good thing about the place was its weather. Warm, yet not scorching like the southern part of the state, and nary a cloud in sight. With mountains to the east and ocean to the west, he had to admit it was a pretty area but not nice enough to set down roots.

They approached one of the countless restaurants, and his stomach rumbled at the appetizing aromas wafting out the window. "How about if we grab a bite to eat, then we can figure out what to do."

"Great idea." She smiled and allowed him to open the door for her. "Mmm. Smells divine in here."

Few of the tables had occupants, and he breathed out a sigh of relief. Had he managed to find the one uncrowded place in San Francisco?

The hostess led them to a table in the far corner, then handed them each a menu. "Your waiter will be here in a moment. Enjoy your meal."

Elijah nodded his thanks, then buried his head in the menu. The prices weren't too bad, but if he and Tegan remained in the city more than a couple of weeks, he'd have to wire for more money. She had offered to help with the expenses, but he refused. He tapped his foot on the floor. Every day they didn't make progress was a day wasted. Fortunately, by all reports, the authorities here were clean and upright men. The fraud apparently hadn't climbed the upper reaches of the government. It might take a while to be seen, but hopefully he could count on a fair and just result.

"Should we check in at the courthouse again tomorrow?" Tegan lowered his menu with one finger and looked over the top. "They said they'd contact us, but maybe they forgot."

"Might be a good idea. It couldn't hurt." He laid down the sheet of paper. "I was surprised to hear about the judge's shooting, but I guess if you have this many people crammed together, you're gonna see all the sins and vices man can dream up."

"True. And fortunately with the number of folks here, there are plenty of lawmen to handle them. Did you hear if they've solved the murder yet?"

"A clerk at the hotel said it has to do with one of the man's old cases: someone he sent to San Quentin. They haven't caught the culprit yet, but they're on his trail."

"So nothing to do with gold claims or possible corruption."

"Nope."

The waiter came, and they gave him their order.

"Food seems mighty expensive here. Are you sure you don't want a contribution?" Tegan cocked her head. "I know you like taking care of everything, but I'm doing well enough to afford adding money to the coffer."

"I'm sure. I'll let you know if I change my mind." He sipped his water. Nice that she didn't expect a free ride. This was the third time she'd offered to pay her way. He might not be fully versed on how to treat a woman, but he did think they should be provided for. She gazed around the room, and he studied her profile. Even after weeks in the sun digging for gold, she was the prettiest woman in the room. Her skin had taken on a tawny color that complemented her honey-brown hair and golden-brown eyes. Her slender form was an intriguing mixture of soft curves and toned muscles.

"Sir?"

Elijah blinked. He'd been so lost in thought he hadn't seen the pair of men approach. Wearing worn but clean clothes, both clutched their hats in gnarled hands. They stood near the table but not so close as to seem a threat. "Yes?"

"Are you Elijah Hunter?" The taller of the two men spoke. "My name's Abe Walesky, and this is Lazor Cholewa."

He frowned at the men. "What's so important that you need to interrupt my dinner?"

"Sorry, sir. We've been looking for a while and got excited to find you." Walesky dipped his head toward Tegan. "My apologies, miss."

Tegan shook her head. "No harm done, gentlemen. How about if you say your piece, but be quick about it."

"Thank you." He licked his lips, then cleared his throat. "We heard you were here to report all the bad goings-on in Nome. We'd like to be part of that."

"How'd you hear about me?" He narrowed his eyes. The men's expressions held no guile, but why would they seek out a man they didn't know to ask for help?

"One of our friends overheard you when you went to the courthouse. They said you seemed real smart and educated." Walesky's cheeks flamed. "And we're not. In fact, most of use can't read, so wrangling the court system is mighty confusing. My friend said you seemed like an honest man."

"He is." Tegan beamed at the man. "Your friend is correct. And we'd be happy to help you."

Elijah rubbed his jaw. "But each person has to make his or her own case."

"Not unless things are different here than in Colorado." Tegan shook her head. "In Boulder, if a bunch of people who had the same legal problem got together, their case held more sway with the judge."

"I don't—"

"Could you at least look into it, sir?"

"I'm just a man like you. No need to call me sir." Elijah tugged at his collar. These men were making him out to be more than he could ever hope to be. "I guess I could look into the possibility of banding together. We were going to the courthouse tomorrow anyway."

Walesky grabbed his hand and pumped it vigorously, then yanked a paper from his shirt pocket. He unfolded it and gave it to Elijah. "Thank you, Mr. Hunter. That means a lot to us. We're staying at the Copper Queen if'n you want to come by and tell us what you find out."

Elijah perused the sheet, his jaw slack. He held it up for Tegan to see. "Twenty men have signed this indicating I'm to speak on their behalf. I hadn't planned to stand up for anyone but you, but I guess I could try." He gaped at the man. "I don't know—"

"We understand the judge might not see fit to let you do this, but we had to try." The man plunked on his hat. "Whenever you come is fine.

No hurry." With that, the two men rushed between the tables and out the door.

Tegan's face shone. "He's right. You're a good man."

His chest swelled. He'd help all of San Francisco if it made her look at him like she was doing at the moment.

Chapter Twenty-One

Heart thundering in her chest, Tegan hurried down the sidewalk next to Elijah. After a fitful night, she'd managed to oversleep, so they'd rushed through breakfast before heading to the courthouse. They turned the corner, and her step faltered. Dozens of men stood in line outside the building waiting to get inside. It was her fault they were late.

"Stop blaming yourself for the crowd." Elijah grabbed her elbow and bent close, speaking in her ear. His breath was warm on her cheek. "There has been a bunch of folks outside every time I've come past."

She nodded, but regret still weighed heavy in her stomach. Squinting against the morning sunlight, she surveyed the group, a typical collection of men wearing scuffed boots, tired-looking clothes, and hats that had seen better days. Not a woman among them, although plenty of ladies were out and about.

With a sigh, she followed Elijah to the back of the line. Not too many of the men stared at her, which was a nice change, and the amount of activity in the area gave her plenty of entertainment to watch while she waited.

Wagons and carriages of all sizes, shapes, and level of affluence rumbled down the street while the sidewalks were packed with pedestrians. Scraps of conversation filtered toward her as families, couples, and the occasional solitary man or woman strolled, strode, or scurried in all directions. The energy was palpable as they went about their business. The town of Boulder would fit in a tiny corner of San Francisco.

Eyes wide, she continued to absorb the scenes playing out before her. A little girl held tight to her mother's hand as she skipped alongside her. The woman glowed as she looked at the child, and a lump formed in Tegan's throat. She couldn't remember her own mother when she was the youngster's age, and despite the love she received from the Llewellyns, moments like this struck hard.

Elijah nudged her forward, and she tore her gaze from the woman, glancing up at him. Concern was etched on his face, and she forced a smile. His look was guarded as he searched her face. "Everything all right?"

"Yes." Eager to divert his attention, she gestured to the thinning crowd. "The line is moving quickly."

"Yep. Shouldn't be too much longer." He shuffled forward as the line moved again, then patted his shirt pocket. "I'm still not sure about representing those men. What if I say or do something wrong?"

"You can only give it your best shot, Elijah. That's all they're—"

"Elijah Hunter?"

Tegan whipped her head toward the voice, and she heard several of the men repeat Elijah's name and point at him. What was going on?

The line parted, and the man motioned toward the entrance of the courthouse. "We heard about what you were doing for Abe and Lazor and some of the others, and we think that's real kind of you. We want to give you first place in line."

"I can't do that. I'll wait my turn. It's not right to cut in."

"No, sir. We all talked about it, and none of us is goin' in until after you."

Her gaze ricocheted around the faces in the crowd, and they all seemed to nod as one at the man's words. She looked at Elijah who seemed stunned and embarrassed at the same time. He was rooted in place, and she looped her hand through his elbow. "Thank you, gentlemen. He'll do the best he can, but makes no promises."

"None expected, miss." The man bobbed his head and gestured to the courthouse again. "Go on, Mr. Hunter."

Elijah shrugged, a look of resignation crossing his features. "Thank you. Good luck with your own case." He walked toward the door, and Tegan gripped his arm as she tried to keep up with his long strides.

They entered the building and followed the signs to the courtroom where the doors were propped open. A lone man sat at a gleaming maple-wood table. Stacks of papers covered the surface as sunlight gleamed through the windows, heating the room. Dressed in a crisply ironed white shirt and charcoal-colored suit, he looked up at the sound of their footfalls.

Fatigue lined his expression, and gray smudges hung below his eyes. "What can I do for you?" His voice bounced off the paneled walls.

As they approached the man, Tegan exchanged a glance with Elijah. If this was the judge, he didn't look nearly as fearful as she'd anticipated. He was reminiscent of her father's business associates in their fine attire and graying hair.

Handing Walesky's paper, her claim, and his to the judge, Elijah bowed slightly. "I'm sure you're busy, Judge, so I'll keep this as short as I can. Miss Llewellyn and I are prospecting in Nome, and we've been told our claims are no good, but we bought them fair and square. There's a judge up there granting fraudulent claims, and we're not going to take that sitting down. That other sheet is from some men who would like me to speak on their behalf, too. That is, if you'll let me. Apparently, their claims have been jumped, too. Can you help us out?"

Silence blanketed the room as the judge studied the papers one at a time. Tegan swallowed a sigh. Could the man hear her heart banging in her chest? Would he grant their request, or would this be a waste of time, money, and effort? Would they be forced to sue, or should they walk away, taking their earnings?

Finally, when she couldn't stand the quiet any longer, the judge scribbled something on the pages, dated and signed his name, then returned the sheaf to Elijah with a tired smile. "We're aware of the shenanigans going on up in Nome, and we're none too happy about it. There are federal agents on their way from Washington, DC to Nome.

They started out a couple of weeks ago. You'll need to hold tight until this judge and his cronies can be arrested, but your claims are valid. They were purchased before he took office. Same can be said for any of the men who bought claims prior to his appointment."

Tegan's breath exploded, and her face warmed. She hadn't realized she'd been holding it. "Thank you, sir."

"Yes, thank you for your time. The men will be pleased."

"I'm afraid the wheels of justice grind slowly, Mr. Hunter, but we will see that the situation is remedied." The judge glanced behind them. "Send in the next man, please."

"Yes, sir." Elijah grinned at Tegan and practically lifted her off her feet as he rushed from the room. They headed out of the building, and he nodded to the first man in line. "The judge will see you." Grinning, he wrapped her in a quick one-armed hug, his face lit up like a Christmas tree. "And you and I are going to celebrate."

Her pulse skittered, and tears prickled the backs of her eyes. They'd agreed to be friends, and nothing more. The worst decision she'd made in a long time. She could no longer deny the fact that she was in love with him. Hopelessly, totally in love with him. And there was nothing she could do about it. She wasn't going to spend her life chasing gold and silver rushes, and he was never going to settle down. It would be unfair to ask him to change just for her. She straightened her spine. "Excellent. Then we can book passage back to Nome."

Where he would eventually leave.

"That's what I love about you, always the planner." Elijah grinned at her, then pressed his lips together. Had she noticed his use of the L word?

She blanched, and his knees nearly buckled. Yep. She'd noticed. He had to steer the conversation in a different direction. "I'm starving. Seeing justice done gets my appetite going. How about this place." He jerked his head toward the nearest restaurant. Had she also noticed he was babbling? She must think him a ninny.

"This place is as good as any, I suppose." She seemed to study his face. "Smells good."

He tugged on her arm, and they ducked inside. Being early for lunch, the place had few patrons, which suited him fine.

A man behind the counter lifted his hand in greeting. "Sit anywhere you want, folks. I'll be right with you."

"Take your time." Elijah's pulse thrummed. Was he brave enough to talk about the elephant in the room? Was this the right place to do it? A nearly empty restaurant seemed better than the hotel lobby, always teeming with guests. He picked a table in the corner. Less chance of being heard. "How about this one?"

"Sure."

He held the chair for her and caught a whiff of her clean scent. His stomach coiled. Maybe getting something to eat wasn't his best idea. He took the chair across from her, then looked up as the man approached and set glasses of water in front of them, then pulled menus from under his arm and laid them on the table.

"Welcome. In addition to my regular fare, I've got chicken and dumplings on special."

"Sounds good to me." Elijah shrugged.

Tegan smiled at the man. "Same for me."

"Good choice. My wife's been working on the recipe for weeks. You're gonna love it." He picked up the menus and wended his way to the kitchen.

She rubbed at the condensation on the glass and stared at the table.

Before he could lose his nerve, Elijah took her hand in his. "Look, about what I said—"

"You were teasing. I get it." Her eyes were cloudy. "You don't have to worry about my feelings."

"I did blurt it out and thought I was kidding, but after I said it, I realized the words were true. I love you."

Tegan gasped and yanked away her hand, then stuffed both hands in her lap.

Reaching down, he laced his fingers with hers, then put their joined hands on the table. "Just hear me out, then you can decide what to do." He swallowed against the lump that had formed in his throat. Man, this was hard. "I didn't set out to fall in love. I wasn't looking for a woman...a wife, but somewhere during all this time together, I've fallen in love with you." He shook his head. "I can't believe how many times I'm saying it. Anyway, you are beautiful and smart and funny, and you laugh at my jokes. But most of all, you have a strong and steadfast faith in God, which makes you beautiful on the inside."

Elijah squeezed her hand. "I know it's a lot to take in, and frankly I'm not sure what to do with my pronouncement either. It's all right if you don't reciprocate. I just wanted you to know how I feel." He sighed. "In fact, why don't we change the subject."

Myriad emotions, including panic, flitted across her face as she stared at him. That was not a good sign.

Chapter Twenty-Two

Elijah's words hung in the air as Tegan's mind raced. He loved her. He actually loved her. Unfeminine, pushy, and overbearing woman that she was, he loved her. How could that be possible? Neither of them was looking for a mate. They each had their own goals and dreams that did not include marriage.

But she loved him, too. With all her being. He was nothing like the men she'd known in Colorado, and he certainly was the antithesis of the slovenly, greedy, and sometimes lustful miners. He made her feel alive in ways she'd never experienced. Challenging her to be a better version of herself.

What should she do with the revelation? She owed him an answer. She'd already taken too long to respond. His face had taken on the look of a puppy who'd been kicked. Nausea threatened to overwhelm her. A husband would ruin everything she'd worked for. Her independence would be gone. She'd be expected to do whatever he told her, right or wrong. Society had no place for a woman with a mind of her own. Even this close to the new century.

"I've obviously offended you, Tegan." He glanced over his shoulder to see if any of the other restaurant patrons were close enough to hear their conversation. "Perhaps I should have told you somewhere else. I'm sorry."

The sound of banging pots came from the kitchen. She took a deep drink of water to coat her parched throat, then set down the glass. "It's me who should be sorry, Elijah. You've bared your heart, and I didn't respond." She pitched her voice low. "The thing is...I love you, too."

His grip on her hand tightened, and his face bloomed with a wide smile. His breath whooshed out. "Oh, Tegan—"

"But we can't do anything about it."

"What?" He released her fingers. Confusion and disappointment warred for supremacy on his face. "You can't mean that."

"I do."

Footsteps approached, and the waiter appeared with their food. He set the plates in front of them with a flourish. "May I get you anything else?"

Elijah shook his head and gave the man a dismissive wave. "We're fine. Thanks."

"Yes, sir." The man bowed, then pivoted and wended his way the kitchen.

Pushing away his dish, Elijah propped his elbows on the table. A deep frown creased his forehead, and his eyes were clouded. "I don't understand. Are you saying we can't pursue a relationship? That I can't court you?"

"That's exactly what I'm saying." She leaned toward him. "We should accept that as wonderful as these feelings are, marriage would never work out for too many reasons to list."

"Try me." His voice was like flint. "I'd appreciate knowing why you think we're a hopeless case."

She slumped in the chair. "We want different things from life. This has been a grand adventure, and I've proven I can make it on my own, but for you chasing the next big rush is your life. I want to put down roots. Maybe in Colorado, but maybe somewhere else. You don't stay in one place for any length of time."

"I was empty inside, Tegan. That's why I was constantly on the move. I had lost sight of what is important: my relationship with God, but also with others. More importantly, with you. With you, I feel like I'm home. I don't need to...what did you say...chase the next rush. We can put down roots wherever you'd like."

"But that could change. You might get bored being in the same place with the same person."

He chuckled. "Life with you would never be boring. Besides, I have thousands of dollars saved. I was fortunate to be highly successful with my prospecting. We can do whatever you want wherever you want."

Warmth spread from her belly to her fingers. He cared enough to change his lifestyle for her. "I've done well, too, but it's not about the riches. I've seen my parents' life, and I want something different. Something more than writing checks or running fundraisers. Philanthropy is important, but it feels empty to me."

"Unsurprising." The worry lines smoothed from his expression. "You're a doer. You took in Gretchen. It's obvious that service is important to you. We can determine what that is." He clasped her fingers, his thumb rubbing circles on the back of her hand. "But we don't have to do it all in one night, or even a week. We're on *your* time schedule, not mine. We'll take this thing at the pace most comfortable for you, but what we have together is special, and I think it's worth pursuing. As you're fond of saying, it's almost a new century. Times are changing, and we don't have to live our lives in a box of someone else's choosing." He released her hand, then picked up his fork and stabbed a chunk of chicken. He winked at her. "Now, enough seriousness. That poor chef went to a lot of trouble to make our dinner. The least we can do is eat it."

She snickered. He always did know how to lighten the mood, and he was right. They were good together. Could they have a marriage that was a partnership? He seemed to accept her as an equal now. Not like when they first met. But who was the real Elijah Hunter? Would he act solicitous and easygoing before they wed, only to revert to a benevolent dictator after they were joined? Her sisters would tell her she was overthinking the issue. But the wrong decision could have dire consequences. Why couldn't she bring herself to trust the man who had stolen her heart?

Chapter Twenty-Three

A stiff breeze tugged at Tegan's hat as the afternoon waned, and she pulled the brim lower on her forehead, then hunched closer to the river. The chilly mid-September air held promises of the upcoming winter. She and Elijah arrived in Nome two days ago after a delightful two weeks on the steamer. The weather had been fine, so the voyage was smooth and easy. They split their time between strolling the deck discussing their dreams and reading aloud to each other. He occasionally helped the crew with their chores. Unlike the journey to San Francisco, the trip home had flown in what seemed like a matter of hours.

Papers from the judge in one hand and gun in the other, Elijah had run off the claim jumpers from both their stakes. The men had been verbally abusive but smart enough not to try anything that might provoke him from using his weapon. As they were slinking away, some of the miners working nearby claims applauded and jeered at the culprits. Hopefully, that was the last they'd see of them, and the agents from Washington would arrive soon to make the arrests as promised.

Gretchen was panning on the beach with her new friends, and Elijah had gone into town to obtain supplies. She'd convinced him she was safe and secure among the prospectors. Besides, her gun was tucked into the back waistband of her denim pants, within easy reach, should the jumpers be foolish enough to come back in broad daylight.

She hummed to herself as she worked. Scoop. Swirl. Tip. Swirl. Pick out the gold flakes. Another few weeks, and it would be time to end the adventure. She'd done well for herself, and Grandmother Hannah would have been proud of her. Mama might be, too, but she rarely said as much. The end of season also meant she needed to make a decision about Elijah.

Elijah.

A sigh escaped as his image washed into her mind. Broad-shouldered and tall, he made her feel petite and feminine. His crystal-blue eyes mesmerized her. Intelligence, wit, and understanding sparkled in his gaze depending on his mood. But it was his spirit that drew her. Tender, but firm. He treated her like a princess yet an equal at the same time, often teasing her that when they got to a big enough town, he'd buy her a tiara. He was the first thing she thought of when she awoke, and the last before falling asleep. Her body trembled when he was near.

But was that enough for her to give up her independence to be with him? Could she trust him to remain as he was today: thoughtful, kind, and attentive? Another sigh, and she pressed her lips together. Gretchen would tell her to pray about the situation.

She had prayed. And prayed. And prayed. But her fears kept getting in the way. God must be tired of her lack of faith. She'd ask Him a question, then go her own way beckoning for Him to keep up.

Another gust of wind buffeted her. "Time to pack it in and make some dinner." She raised her chin and surveyed the area, but Elijah was nowhere in sight. How long did it take to grab what they needed and return? Maybe his true colors were seeping out, and he was enjoying one or more of the vices offered in town.

Dusk was coming quickly, purple and pink streaks darkening the sky. With fluid motions, she collected her tools and stuffed them into her duffel bag. She climbed to her feet, then slung the strap over her shoulder, and trudged toward the rows of tents that dotted the hillside. She'd been spoiled by the days in the San Francisco hotel where she'd slept in a real bed with walls and a door. Her next exploit would *not* include lodging in a canvas shelter.

Tegan shouldered past the flap and into her tent. She dropped the satchel in the corner, then grabbed a biscuit left over from breakfast and a couple of strips of jerky. Not exceptionally appetizing, nonetheless, the food would assuage her hunger without the need of building a fire.

Rustling sounded on the other side of the canvas, and she grinned as her pulse quickened. Elijah had returned. She headed outside. "It's about—"

Two men pointed guns at her in the growing darkness. "One scream or shout, and we'll kill you. Understand?"

Her gaze ricocheted between their weapons and their faces. She recognized both of them. The jumpers had come back. She straightened her spine and brought her fists to her hips. Hopefully, she looked braver than she felt. "What do you want?" She spoke through gritted teeth.

"What do you think?" The beefier of the two men sneered and gestured with the weapon. "You made two mistakes: coming to Alaska in the first place, then going to San Francisco to bring the law down on us. You're in the way, and we plan to correct that." An ugly laugh rumbled in his chest. "Should have listened to your boyfriend and left when you had the chance. He should have, too. Now it's too late for both of you."

A chill swept over Tegan, and she swallowed a sob. Had they killed Elijah? Is that why he hadn't returned from town? Her chin quivered. *Is this how I'm going to die, Lord? Far from home and alone? Why did you let Elijah and I fall in love if You were going to let us get killed?*

"Here's how it's gonna work. You're gonna head up the hill, and we'll be right behind you, so don't try any funny stuff, or we'll fill ya full of holes. We got horses waiting to make our escape." He gave her an evil grin. "You'll ride with me."

She shuddered, and her stomach roiled, threatening to return the biscuit. She had to stall them. Make them wait until one or more of the miners wandered back to their tents. Would they come to her aid if they thought she was in peril? "Where are we going?"

"You'll see when we get there." He motioned with the gun again. "Get moving."

On wooden legs, she stumbled forward. He moved close, gripped her elbow with one hand, and pressed the muzzle of the gun against her with the other. They marched between the tents, then climbed the hill, the ground course and uneven under her feet. What could she do to leave a trail? Would anyone even look for her, or would they assume she'd left on her own accord?

Remembering the handkerchief in her pocket, she stilled. She could drop that, then maybe the ribbon that held her braid. What else did she have?

The cold steel seeped through her shirt. "Quit dallying and get on the horse."

"All right." She pretended to struggle, then yanked out the hanky and let go of it. It fluttered downward to the ground, stark white against the dark ground. Her heart hammered. Would her captors see it and know what she was doing? Shoving her foot into the stirrup, she swung herself onto the horse, and the man quickly mounted behind her. He seemed oblivious to the discarded scrap of material. Perhaps she had a chance after all.

Chapter Twenty-Four

"Elijah!"

He bolted upright on the cot inside his tent. "Gretchen?"

"Yes. Please come. I think something has happened to Tegan." Her voice quavered. "She's missing."

"What?" He snatched the shirt from the end of the bed and yanked on the garment, then threw back the covers and swung his feet to the ground. "I'll be right there." His fingers fumbled with the buttons, but he finally managed to get the shirt closed.

She sniffled. "All right."

He shoved one leg into his pants, then the other before brushing the dirt from his feet and putting on his socks and boots. Tegan gone? *Please, God, keep her safe and help me find her if she's truly missing.* His heart thundered in his chest. Where could she be? Grabbing his hat, he clamped it on his head and rushed outside.

Gretchen stood nearby wringing her hands. Tears had streaked her wan face. "I'm sorry to bother you, but I didn't know where to turn."

"It's no bother. Of course, you should have sought me out." He forced himself to breathe slowly. Tegan might have simply gone into town. He grasped her shoulders. "Tell me why you think something's happened?"

"We agreed to have breakfast together this morning, but when I got to her tent, she wasn't there, and the bed hadn't been slept in. I checked her claim, and she's not at the river."

"It'd be unusual, but maybe she stayed in town last night."

"No, she didn't say anything about that, and she would have told me." She poked her toe in the soil and ducked her head. "Don't laugh, but it didn't look right, you know, inside her tent. Not exactly like there was a struggle, but she's neat as a pin, and there were items lying about. Even if she did go to town, she wouldn't have left her place a mess."

A chill slithered up Elijah's spine. Gretchen was right. He'd noticed Tegan's fastidiousness and admired her for keeping the rustic shelter tidy in the midst of the wilderness. If the canvas lodge was unkempt, Tegan was in trouble. "You did right to tell me. I will find her, but I need you to pray as hard as you can that God will lead me to her."

Gretchen nodded, her eyes shimmering with tears. "Thank you for believing me," she whispered.

"Every time, Gretchen." He pulled her into a quick hug. "She's blessed to call you friend and have you looking out for her. I'll go into town and talk to the sheriff. He's been as crooked as a dog's back leg, but maybe he'll do the right thing. You can pray about that, too."

Looking forlorn, she nodded and wrapped her arms around her middle. "I'll be in her tent until you return."

With a curt nod, he headed toward the river where many prospectors were already hunched over the water. He crouched next to the first man he came to. "By any chance, have you seen Miss Llewellyn?"

The man glared at him and shook his head.

"Sorry to bother you." Elijah stood and marched to the next miner. "Have you seen Miss Llewellyn?"

"Nope." The man continued to pan without looking up.

Elijah gritted his teeth and went to another man, then another. No one had seen her. He growled in frustration.

"Hey, mister." A few yards away, a young man who looked no more than twenty waved at him. "You looking for that lady with the shiny brown hair? Always wears it in a braid?"

"Yes! Have you seen her?"

"Yeah, last night just as it was getting dark, her and some guy headed out of camp. She didn't look too happy, and they rode double on a roan."

His heart stuttered. Had she been kidnapped? The Tegan he knew would want her own horse. "What direction did they go?"

The man jerked his head toward the east end of camp.

"Thanks. You've been a big help. Elijah raced back to the tent city and grabbed his tack from inside his place, then rushed up the hill to the lean-to where the horses and mules were housed. Willing his fingers to work, he saddled his gelding and fitted the bit into the horse's mouth. He jumped onto the animal's back and swung him toward town. "Come on, Sergeant. Tegan needs our help."

Kneeing the horse forward, Elijah bent low over the gelding's neck. He shoved aside images of what the man might do to her. *God, give her peace and keep her from harm. Lead me to her, Father.* He leaned closer to Sergeant's ear. "Faster, boy, our girl needs us." The horse surged forward, and his hooves reverberated on the dry ground. They arrived in front of the jailhouse, and Elijah reined in the animal. He jumped from his back and tied the traces around the rail, then raced inside.

"Sheriff, I need your help."

A bearlike man with a shock of black hair, Floyd Sawyer had taken the job of sheriff after his brother was killed in a brawl at the beginning of the rush. Initially, he'd tamed the town, but rumor had it he'd gotten into debt and began to take bribes as a way out of his financial straits. He probably received a nice chunk of change to look the other way when the claim jumpers came calling and the judge started handing out fake validations.

Sawyer's face darkened, and he jumped up from his chair. "What's wrong with you, banging in here like a crazy man?"

Rather than bark at the man which might have the opposite effect of what he needed, Elijah took a deep break and drew himself to his full height, towering over the man. "Tegan Llewellyn has been kidnapped."

The man's eyebrows shot to his hairline, then he schooled his features to look nonchalant. "What makes you say that? She probably got tired of playing in the mud and took yesterday's steamer out of here."

"Not a chance. I saw her yesterday afternoon. And her friend, Gretchen Quirke, has reported her missing. A witness says she left camp riding double with some man."

A deep chuckle resounded in Sawyer's chest, and his face took on a lecherous expression. "Well, it sounds like she's just off to have a good time. I'd heard she was a goody-two-shoes. Guess she's not more than a camp follower after all."

Elijah clenched his fists and stifled the desire to punch the man. "She's not a camp follower. She's a believer in God and wouldn't ride off in the woods with a man. She also owns a horse and wouldn't ride double with anyone. Her place is a mess, which isn't like her. Now, are you going to help me find her, or can you deputize me so I can do it on my own?"

"You're serious, ain't you?"

"Yes!" Elijah yanked off his hat and raked his fingers through his hair. "You think I would pull a prank like this? What kind of sheriff are you?"

The man's eyebrows came together. "One who's seen a lot of nonsense in this town. And drunks who say and do stupid things."

"Well, I'm not drunk, and this isn't nonsense."

"Okay, simmer down. I'll help you, but I'll deputize you, too. Just in case things get ugly, and we gotta use weapons." Sawyer cleared his throat. "Raise your right hand and repeat what I say."

Elijah lifted his hand and parroted the words given by the sheriff. Seconds later, they were out the door and mounted. Would he find Tegan in time?

Chapter Twenty-Five

Tugging at her bonds, Tegan winced as the rope cut into her wrists that her abductor bound behind her. Her ankles were tied to the front legs of the sturdy wooden chair where he'd shoved her after they'd arrived. The guy wasn't the sharpest knife in the drawer, but he knew how to hogtie. In her mouth, the bandanna the man had used to gag her was filthy, tasting of dirt, sweat, and too many other foul items to consider.

After he'd gone outside, she'd attempted to break the chair, to no avail. Why couldn't the chair be as rickety as the rest of the decrepit-looking furniture in the dilapidated cabin? He was talking to a man she hadn't seen yet, so apparently there were at least two involved in the scheme. But why kidnap her? Not that she wanted to be dead, but he could have shot her, then taken the claim.

Father, I'm in dire straits right now, and I'm trying not to panic. You knew this would happen and what will happen. I know You're in control, but it's hard not to be scared. Her lips trembled. *Elijah's dead, and I messed up. Making him wait for my decision wasn't fair, and now it's too late. Please save me.*

Her captors' voices were muffled, and she strained her ears to try to catch their conversation. Fortunately, there were plenty of cracks in the tiny shack, allowing their words to filter inside.

"Did ya bring food with ya?"

"Nah, we ain't gonna be here more than a couple of days, and we got plenty." Her kidnapper's voice was slurred. Had they begun to drink? Would that give her a chance to escape?

"I'm tired of jerky and hardtack."

"Well, unless'n you're hiding something in your saddlebags, that's our choice. Besides, I don't want to draw attention to us, and a fire would do that."

"Fine, but when this is all over, we're gonna get some real food." Nasal and twangy, the words also held a touch of whining.

"Whatever. But it can't be over too soon for me."

Rolling her eyes, Tegan strained against the ropes again. As frightened as she was, the argument over food was amusing, but what did they have planned in two days' time? Is that when they'd kill her? Or were they just holding her for someone more important, like the judge? She needed to get away.

"Why can't we swap her tomorrow? Why wait?"

"Because I want to scare that man into doin' what we ask. He loves this gal, and if'n he's gotta wait to see her, he'll be more likely to give us his claim."

Tegan froze. Were they talking about Elijah? Was he alive? Had her abductor lied when he insinuated he'd killed him? *Please, God, let it be true.* Her heart lightened. If he was alive, he'd come after her. He'd never let these men get away with snatching her.

"I think we should ask for money, you know. What do they call it?"

"A ransom?"

"Yeah, that might be better for us. It's getting too hot to stay here ever since folks started going to court in San Francisco. Why work a claim when we can take the money and run?"

"You might be onto something." A sinister laugh accompanied his words. "Hmm. The more I think about it, the more I like that idea, but we're supposed to just hold her until we get word that things have been taken care of."

"But if we do it quick-like, we can be out of town before anyone's the wiser."

"Let me think on it."

"What's there to think about? I'm sick of being stuck up here. I wanna get back to California where there are easier ways to make money than digging in the river or ocean. And there ain't enough women in Nome. Not yet, anyway."

"We got us one in the cabin." Another evil laugh sounded. "How's that strike you?"

Nausea rolled over Tegan, and she swallowed against the sour rag in her mouth. She would not stay and let them have their way with her. Not while there was still breath within her. She leaned to the side trying to get the chair to tip over. Nothing. Pushing with her right foot, she strained to get off-balance enough to fall to the ground. Still nothing.

She growled, then jerked her body to the left, and the chair teetered for a long moment before crashing to the floor. Pain shot up her shoulder, wrist, and knee, and she nearly groaned. The chair remained intact.

The door slammed open, and her captors ran inside. The man who'd grabbed her from camp snarled, "Nice try, little lady." He jerked his head toward the other man, and they lifted the chair back on its legs. "You know if you make too much trouble, it might be easier to kill you."

Sheriff Sawyer had proven himself an adept tracker. Granted, Tegan's captors hadn't done much to hide their trail, but there were a few times the sheriff had to work to find the path. They'd stumbled on the crumbling cabin about ten minutes ago. Backtracking a hundred yards or so, they tied their horses to a couple of trees so they wouldn't be heard in case they whinnied, then returned to the edge of the clearing. Who had built a shack this deep in the forest? And why had they vacated it?

"We need to get the lay of the land, see what they're doing inside and if there are more of them. There are only two horses, so I'm hoping the two varmints we saw are the only ones here.

Elijah pursed his lips. "They ran inside like something was up. Did you hear the crash?"

A crooked grin eased the lines on the lawman's face. "Maybe your girl is giving them what for. She might be trying to escape."

"That could get her killed."

"Yep, unless they're holding her for someone else."

"Who?"

Sawyer shrugged. "Can you think of anybody who'd want to do her or you harm? Revenge?"

"Sure, those guys who tried to jump our claim."

"I don't know. Most jumpers wouldn't stoop to kidnapping. If they couldn't grab one stake, they'd try getting another one. You sure there's not someone out to do you wrong?"

"Not that I can think of."

"All right. Well, you stay here, and I'm gonna circle around behind the cabin and get the lay of the land, see where the windows are, and count the scoundrels. Need to know if we're over our heads." He pointed at Elijah. "You sit tight until I get back. Don't go trying to be a hero."

"Not unless you need rescuing." Elijah nudged the man's shoulder. Whatever his faults and sins, he seemed intent on helping Tegan.

"Funny. I was raised by a daddy who'd sooner hit me than hug me, so I've got all kinds of tricks up my sleeve." He unholstered his gun, then crept forward.

Elijah watched until he disappeared from view. Silence descended as if even the birds and critters held their breath. His chest tightened, and he rubbed his sternum. *I know You're in control, Father, but I'm feeling mighty scared right now. Tegan must be, too. Help the sheriff and me, and I'd rather not kill anyone in the process. Or get killed.*

Peace wrapped around him like a warm blanket, and he smiled. *Thank You, Lord.*

Minutes passed, and Elijah's legs cramped from squatting. He shifted his feet. Branches snapped, and he gulped. Could they hear that? Would they think it was man or beast? The door to the cabin closed with a bang. Were they doing that to hole up or just keep her inside?

More time crawled by, then suddenly Sawyer appeared. "There's just two of 'em like we hoped, and Tegan is creating problems." He snickered. "She's definitely more than they bargained for."

"That's my girl." He grinned, then sobered. "What's your plan?"

Sawyer outlined what he thought they should do to catch the kidnappers off guard, Elijah nodding as the lawman spoke. "They don't seem too worried about being found. Neither one is wearing or carrying a weapon."

"Really? That seems too easy."

"Yep, but maybe all that prayin' you've been doin' is working. I don't know how your God works, but it seems like He's making them stupid."

"I'm not sure how He works, either, but I believe He's here."

"That's what counts. When this is over, you can tell me more about Him." Sawyer rose and gestured with his gun. They crept through the woods, walking on the balls of their feet trying to avoid fallen branches that might make noise. When they arrived parallel to the cabin, Sawyer ducked and sped across the clearing. He made it to the shack without being seen and pressed himself against the decaying wood. He tiptoed until he was next to the first window, then gestured for Elijah to make his move.

Heart in his throat, Elijah pulled out his pistol, mimicked Sawyer's posture, and lowered himself into a crouch before running toward the porch. Panting, he inched toward the door. Ear to the wood, he strained to hear.

Glass shattered, and Sawyer shouted, "Hands up, boys, you're surrounded."

Elijah kicked open the door and pointed his gun at the men. Sawyer's weapon was poking through the hole he'd made, his face lit like a boy on his birthday. He was apparently enjoying getting back to being a real lawman.

The men scowled and swore.

"Hey, not in front of a lady." Continuing to point his pistol at the captors, Elijah eased his way to Tegan.

"Watch these varmints. I'll be right there." Sawyer disappeared and, a moment later, barreled through the door. "I've got these guys. You untie your lady." He dipped his head to Tegan. "Nice to see you again, Miss Llewellyn."

Dropping to his knees, Elijah holstered his gun, then wrenched on the knots binding her wrists. When she was free, she flung her arms around him and buried her face in his neck. He stroked her hair, murmuring assurances that she was safe, and he would never let anything happen to her again. She finally released him, and he untied her legs. He helped her stand. She wobbled, and he wrapped his arm around her waist.

"Give me a minute, and I'll get my feet under me."

"You were very brave."

Her cheeks pinked, and she ducked her head.

"Well, ain't this a happy reunion." The shorter of the two men twisted his lips. "If you're gonna take us in, can we get on with it?"

"Shut yer yap." Sheriff Sawyer poked him with the muzzle of his gun. "Hunter's gonna tie you up, and if you so much as flinch, I'll make sure you never flinch again. Shame on you, kidnapping a lady. You deserve whatever the courts throw at you."

"I'd like to do the honors if you'll let me, Sheriff," Tegan said.

Elijah guffawed. "Guess you've met your match, boys." He released her. "And when we get these guys behind bars, you and I have a lot to talk about."

She brushed her lips against his, then whispered in his ear, "You mean like where we're going to get married?"

December 31, 1899, just before midnight
Boulder, Colorado

Epilogue

A Debussy waltz filled the air, and couples whirled around her parent' ballroom as Tegan tried to focus on the inane chatter of the ladies surrounding her. Elijah was hidden among the circle of tuxedoed men across the room, but he periodically winked at her over the heads of his companions, making her pulse race. Tonight was the first time she'd seen him in a suit, and she'd nearly swooned when he'd appeared at her door to escort her downstairs. He was a gorgeous man in flannel and jeans, but the tux rendered him even more devastatingly handsome.

The three and a half months since being rescued had flown in the blink of an eye—cliché, but true. Her abductors had been trussed up like turkeys, then tied to their horses with a threat from the sheriff to shoot them if they tried to get away. The journey back to Nome had been long and tedious, but they'd finally arrived. She gave her statement, then Elijah insisted on putting her up in the hotel where he'd sat guard outside her door all night.

She'd taken a luxurious bath, then slept until noon the following day. The place wasn't fancy, but it was clean and a whole lot better than the cot in her tent. They'd dawdled over a lunch of steak, mashed potatoes, and glazed carrots. After sharing a slice of decadent chocolate cake, Elijah got out of his chair, dropped to one knee, and proposed. Without hesitation, she'd accepted, and in a matter of minutes, she would become Mrs. Hunter.

As she watched, he extricated himself from the men and strolled across the floor in her direction. Her pulse sped up, and the chaos of the room faded. His eyes glittered with heat as they met hers. She extricated herself from the women and glided toward him, her skirts swishing around her legs. With a saucy grin, she said, "Good evening, Mr. Hunter. Are you enjoying yourself?"

He slid one arm around her waist and leaned closed to her ear. "Not as much as I will be soon."

"Shame on you." Her cheeks scorched, and she swatted him. A deep chuckle resonated in his chest. "Life with you won't be boring."

"That's my plan." He waggled his eyebrows, then pulled her into his arms and onto the dance floor. "This is the only legal way I'm able to embrace you at the moment."

"You really must behave."

She giggled at his unsuccessful attempt to look contrite. "You're a wicked man."

"Which is why you love me." With smooth motions, he twirled her, then brought her back into his arms, the warmth of his body seeping through her dress.

"One of many reasons." Her smile faltered. "Thank you for not giving up on me. In an odd way, I'm grateful for being captured. The incident made me see that I couldn't live without you."

"I wish there had been an easier way for you."

"Sometimes God has to use *unusual* ways to get our attention." She shuddered. "From now on, I'll pay better attention to Him so He doesn't have to employ such extreme measures."

Another chuckle. "And I'll be there to keep you safe."

"Wherever we might be."

Uncertainty clouded his eyes. "Are you sure you want to travel part of each year? You want roots."

"I realized home is not so much a place as a feeling, and when we're together, I'm plenty rooted."

"Ten...nine..." Someone in the crowd started the countdown. "Eight...seven...six...five..." Others joined in. "Four...three...two...one! Happy New Year!"

The band broke into a rousing rendition of "Auld Lang Syne," and a few folks sang along.

"Happy New Year, my love." Elijah lowered his head and pressed his lips on hers.

Tingles shot to the tips of her fingers, and her toes curled as she trembled in his arms. The man made her as weak-kneed as a newborn colt. She'd journey to the ends of the earth if he asked. "Happy New Year."

Shouts and singing continued as they reveled in each other's presence, then clapping sounded, and the noise ceased.

"Happy New Year, everyone." Her father stood in front of the small orchestra, his hands in the air. "Thank you for helping us celebrate our entry into the new century, but more importantly, for joining us to witness the joyous occasion of our daughter's wedding." He beckoned to her and Elijah. "Which I'm sure these two are anxious to begin. So, if everyone will move toward the walls, we'll get started."

Elijah laced his fingers with hers and squeezed her hand as they walked to the center of the room where the minister waited next to her parents. Her father kissed her cheek, then gripped Elijah's shoulder for a quick moment. "Take care of my little girl."

"That's my plan, sir."

Mama gave her a watery smile and drew her into an embrace. "I'm thrilled for you. Elijah is a wonderful man." Her mother whispered, "And quite the looker."

Tegan gasped, then giggled. She'd never seen her mother so lighthearted, and she enjoyed this new side of her.

"Enough talk. Let's get you married." Her mother moved to her husband's side, sliding her hand through the crook of his arm. He gave her a dazzling smile, causing her to blush.

Would Elijah look at her like that after thirty years of marriage?

"Yes."

"What?" She turned to him.

"Yes," He murmured close to her ear. "I'll still look at you like that when we're old and gray." He kissed her cheek.

"Young man, you're jumping the gun." The minister wagged his finger at Elijah and gave him an exaggerated frown.

Laughter swept the room, and Elijah grinned. "Guess I'm just anxious to start my new life with this lady."

Tegan sighed. What a life it would be.

THE END

What did you think of *Gold Rush Bride Tegan?*

Thank you so much for purchasing *Gold Rush Bride Tegan.* You could have selected any number of books to read, but you chose this book.

I hope it added encouragement and exhortation to your life. If so, it would be nice if you could share this book with your family and friends by posting to one or more of your favorite social media outlets.

If you enjoyed this book and found some benefit in reading it, I'd appreciate it if you could take some time to post a review on Amazon, Goodreads, BookBub, or other book review site of your choice. Your feedback and support will help me to improve my writing craft for future projects and make this book even better.

Thank you again for your purchase.

Blessings,
Linda Shenton Matchett

Want more *Gold Rush Brides?* See where the story began with *Gold Rush Bride Hannah*

Chapter One

Reverberations from the gunshot echoed among the hills surrounding Hannah Lauman's property as she gripped the rifle and watched the cougar disappear through the trees. Winter had apparently not been kind to the gaunt and shaggy animal, prompting its boldness to approach the homestead. Fortunately, Quinn had taught her to shoot, so she could protect herself during the times he was away from their claim. Four-legged beasts weren't the only predators she'd had to scare off after word got out about how much gold she and her husband were pulling from Yahoola Creek.

Despite a chilly gust that tugged at her skirt, perspiration trickled down her spine and pooled under her arms. No matter how often she used a gun, she'd never get used to the thunderous boom or the weapon's kick against her shoulder. She'd sport a bruise by nightfall. She reloaded the rifle, then leaned the gun against the clothes line post. Next to the basket filled with wet laundry. She needed to be ready if the big cat decided to return. Would she ever get used to living so remotely?

Hannah wiped the sweat off her forehead with her sleeve, then blew out a deep breath. Philosophizing over her lot in life wouldn't get the chores done, and she had plenty to complete before Quinn's return by dinner, provided he wasn't late. Some women had to worry about their husbands' penchants for drinking, gambling, and other detrimental pursuits, but Quinn's worst habit was getting caught up in the beauty of the outdoors and losing track of time.

Panning this week had been more productive than usual and storing the accumulated flakes and nuggets in the cabin was never a good idea, so today's journey to Gainesville was his third trip to the bank. How long the gold would hold out was anyone's guess, so she should probably be down at the water's edge, but the two of them were out of clean clothes, and she hadn't swept or dusted in days. She wasn't so gold-hungry that she'd live in a pigsty.

She grabbed one of Quinn's shirts and hung the cotton garment over the line, then bent and picked up another. She ought to warn the other miners about the wildcat, but perhaps the gunshot would bring one of the neighbors running so she wouldn't have to seek them out. She continued to hang the laundry, periodically glancing over her shoulder in case the cougar decided to return. Known for their humanlike screams, the tawny cats crept with silent stealth when on the prowl.

Finished with the clothes, she gave one last look toward the forest, then picked up the basket and headed toward the cabin. Inside, she lit one of the lamps to push away the gloom from the small abode. She'd put her foot down when Quinn suggested they build a soddy, but some days the tiny two-room abode didn't seem much better. With only one small window next to the door, the interior remained dim except on the sunniest of days.

"Hello, the house." A shrill voice sounded in the yard.

Hannah stepped to the doorway and waved.

Glenda Thompson, the wife of another miner a few claims away waddled toward her, the woman's swollen stomach evidence of her late-term pregnancy. She carried a towel-wrapped bundle. "Good afternoon, Hannah. I made several loaves of bread and thought y'all might be able to use one."

"Real bread sounds heavenly. We've been eating biscuits with most of our meals. Quinn will be thrilled."

The petite blonde woman handed her the loaf, then rested her arms on her belly. "Where is that husband of yours? I didn't see him on my way over. Thought he'd be down at the water with the rest of the boys sifting through the sand."

"He went into Gainesville. Should be back any time."

"Another trip to the bank?" Glenda's eyebrow lifted. "Y'all must be doin' better than the rumors say."

Hannah shrugged. "Quinn's no Stephen Girard. We won't be financing the government any time soon."

Glenda giggled, then sighed. "At least you're gettin' by."

"Not quite the thrills and riches we were promised, huh?" Hannah tucked a stray hair behind her ear. "We've done better than some, but the work is backbreaking, and the worry about claim jumpers, injury, and wildlife is wearing." She snapped her fingers. "By the way, a cougar wandered into the yard a short time ago. You might have heard the gunshot."

"I thought Quinn might be huntin' squirrels or rabbits. That's bad news about the wildcat. I'll be sure to pass the word." Glena huffed out a breath. "You ever wonder what life would be like if you weren't diggin' for gold day in and day out?"

"More often than you'd think." She gestured to the garments flapping on the line. "If you'd have been here earlier, you'd have heard me arguing with myself. Like I said, we're doing all right, but I miss the conveniences we had in Atlanta as well as the socializing. It gets lonely." Especially with no children, but Hannah wouldn't get into that. Married for nearly ten years, she'd yet to conceive. And the longer her childlessness went on, the farther apart she and Quinn grew. She shook her head to clear the morose thoughts. "Everything, okay?"

"We've about played out our claim. Might be movin' on." Glenda's chin trembled. "There are a few claims available up rifer, so Bart's thinkin' of buying one of those. This was going to be our chance to get ahead. Scrimpin' by on a blacksmith's income before comin' here was better than this. I'm not sure how much more gold chasin' I can do, but Bart doesn't listen to me. He's sure we're gonna strike it big."

"He might not be wrong. Quite a few claims have produced significantly." Hannah rocked on her heels. "We only found dribs and drabs when we first arrived. We kept at it, and finally hit a good vein."

"Yeah, but we're gonna have a family to think about soon. We need a stable salary." Glenda rubbed the cross dangling from a long silver chain around her neck. "I've been prayin' Bart will come to his senses, but nothin' yet."

"I'm sorry things are hard for you." Hannah fiddled with the edge of the towel. If their claim hadn't produced, would Quinn have been willing to walk away? Go back to their staid life in the city? If truth be told, they'd done better working the gold. A bit of a dreamer, he'd held and lost numerous jobs over the course of their lives together, always moving on to opportunities that were supposed to be bigger and better. The day he'd come home and announced he'd purchased a gold claim from a widow, they'd argued well into the night. Then she'd decided that working together might sweeten their marriage, draw them close again. She was still waiting for that to happen. *What was it with me and their desire for fortune and glory?*

Thundering hooves pounded, and Hannah's head whipped toward the sound. Chet Fawley, Dahlonega's sheriff crouched low over his horse's neck. He brought the animal to a halt, then slid from the saddle. His face was lined with fatigue and sadness.

Hannah's stomach hollowed, and her hand flew to her throat. There was no doubt the man brought bad news. "Quinn?" Her lips moved, but no sound came out.

Sheriff Fawley removed his dusty Stetson and licked his lips. "I'm sorry, Miz Lauman. Your husband's dead. Ambushed outside of town."

Dizziness struck, and she swayed. Glenda wrapped her arm around Hannah's shoulder, keeping her from falling to the ground in a heap. Dots of light danced in her vision, and roaring, like an approaching train, filled her ears. A lump formed in her throat. "Ambushed?" Her voice caught, and she swallowed. "Who would want to murder my husband?"

"Looks like the work of the Cherokees. I've got my boys looking into things as we speak." He ducked his head. "I guess you'll be pulling out and going back to Atlanta, so be sure to let me know how to contact you when I solve the case. Shouldn't be long."

Overhead, the sun broke out from behind a bank of clouds casting a bright beam onto Hannah's face. A slight breeze brushed her cheeks as if God had reached down to remind her of His love and presence, even during this terrible turn of events. Hannah squared her shoulders. "I'm not going anywhere, Sheriff, I've got a claim to work."

Acknowledgments

Although writing a book is a solitary task, it is not a solitary journey. There have been many who have helped and encouraged me along the way.

My parents, Richard and Jean Shenton, who presented me with my first writing tablet and encouraged me to capture my imagination with words. Thanks, Mom and Dad!

Scribes212 – my ACFW online critique group: Valerie Goree, Marcia Lahti, and the late Loretta Boyett (passed on to Glory, but never forgotten). Without your input, my writing would not be nearly as effective.

Eva Marie Everson – my mentor/instructor with Christian Writers' Guild. You took a timid, untrained student and turned her into a writer. Many thanks!

SincNE, and the folks who coordinate the Crimebake Writing Conference. I have attended many writing conferences, but without a doubt, Crimebake is one of the best. The workshops, seminars, panels, critiques, and every tiny aspect are well-executed, professional, and educational.

Special thanks to Hank Phillippi Ryan, Halle Ephron, and Roberta Isleib for your encouragement and spot-on critiques of my work.

Paula Proofreader (https://paulaproofreader.wixsite.com/home): I'm so glad I found you! My work is cleaner because of your eagle eye. Any mistakes are completely mine.

Thanks to my Book Brigade who provide information, encouragement, and support.

A heartfelt thank you to my brothers, Jack Shenton and Douglas Shenton, and my sister, Susan Shenton Greger for being enthusiastic cheerleaders during my writing journey. Your support means more than you'll know.

My husband, Wes, deserves special kudos for understanding my need to write. Thank you for creating my writing room – it's perfect, and I'm thankful for it every day. Thank you for your willingness to accept a house that's a bit cluttered, laundry that's not always done, and meals on the go. I love you.

And finally, to God be the glory. I thank Him for giving me the gift of writing and the inspiration to tell stories that shine the light on His goodness and mercy.

Other Titles by this Author

Romance
Love's Harvest, Wartime Brides, Book 1
Love's Rescue, Wartime Brides, Book 2
Love's Belief, Wartime Brides, Book 3
Love's Allegiance, Wartime Brides, Book 4

Spies & Sweethearts, Sisters in Service, Book 1
The Mechanic & The MD, Sisters in Service, Book 2
The Widow & The War Correspondent, Sisters in Service, Book 3

Gold Rush Bride Hannah, Gold Rush Brides, Book 1
Gold Rush Bride Caroline, Gold Rush Brides, Book 2
Gold Rush Bride Tegan, Gold Rush Brides, Book 2

Dinah's Dilemma, Westward Home & Hearts Mail Order Brides
Rayne's Redemption, Westward Home & Hearts Mail Order Brides
Daria's Duke, Westward Home & Hearts Mail Order Brides
Ellie's Escape, Westward Home & Hearts Mail Order Brides

Vanessa's Replacement Valentine, Brides of Pelican Rapids
A Family for Hazel, Brides of Pelican Rapids

Legacy of Love, Keepers of the Light

A Bride for Seamus, Proxy Bride Series
A Bride for Keegan, Proxy Bride Series

Estelle's Endeavor, Thanksgiving Books & Blessings Series

Love at First Flight
Love Found in Sherwood Forest
On the Rails: A Harvey Girls Story
A Love Not Forgotten

A Doctor in the House

Mystery
Under Fire, Ruth Brown Mystery Series, Book 1
Under Cover, Ruth Brown Mystery Series, Book 2
Under Ground, Ruth Brown Mystery Series, Book 3

Murder of Convenience, Women of Courage, Book 1
Murder at Madison Square Garden, Women of Courage, Book 2

Non-Fiction
WWII Word Find, Volume 1

Let's Connect!

www.LindaShentonMatchett.com

www.facebook.com/LindaShentonMatchettAuthor

www.pinterest.com/lindasmatchett

www.linkedin.com/in/authorlindamatchett

https://www.amazon.com/Linda-Shenton-Matchett/e/B01DNB54S0

https://www.bookbub.com/authors/linda-shenton-matchett

https://www.youtube.com/@lindamatchett

Interested in more historical fiction?
Visit http://www.lindashentonmatchett.com/p/books.html